REFUGE LIFE & HOME

MICHAEL ALLEN GEORGE

ISBN 978-1-64133-852-3 (softcover)
ISBN 978-1-64133-853-0 (ebook)

This book is a work of fiction. Names, characters, places, and incidents are the product of the author's imagination or are used fictitiously. Any resemblance to actual locales, events, or persons, living or dead, is purely coincidental.

Printed in the United States of America.

Brilliant Books Literary
137 Forest Park Lane Thomasville
North Carolina 27360 USA

This book is respectfully dedicated to

Jim Von Meyer
and
Bonnie Haubenschild

They were there at the end
When it mattered so much

Books by Michael George

The Refuge Mystery Series

Why A Refuge	Book One
Bridge To No Good	Book Two
Grass Was Greener	Book three
To Save The Refuge	Book Four
Without Refuge	Book five
Refuge Of Another Kind	Book Six
Places Of Refuge	Book Seven
Refuge Life And Home	Book Eight

Other Books By Michael George

Horses Lemons And Pretty Girls
More Horses And Pretty Girls
Finding Peri Gray
Of Rain Barrels And Bridges

Books Written With Bud George And David George

Stories From Three Brothers
More Stories From Three Brothers

Books written as Michael Allen George

Why A Refuge
Places Of Refuge
Refuge Life And Home

PROLOGUE

I t was a terrible winter, with extreme cold and snowfall. When the spring thaw finally came, there was record snow on the ground. The warm weather came fast and continued, causing the snow to melt as fast as anyone could remember. With the ground still frozen solid, the melting snow couldn't soak into the ground, so nearly all of it ran off into the rivers. Along with that, came a steady rain. It was perfect conditions for flooding.

Among the many rivers over flowing their banks was the always rather docile, slow moving St. Catherine river. This spring, she was an angry torrent with over flowing banks. She was higher than what was ever previously recorded, causing all the lakes and ponds within its boundaries to overflow, even though they had nearly dried up during the previous years drought.

Upstream of the now private wildlife refuge it was much the same. Many of the small farms along its banks were now under water, as were all of the many lowlands.

In the farm house of one of the larger farms of the area, two young girls watched the water rise. They were locked inside the house, with access only to the main living area. The exterior door was steel and deadbolt locked. It was a replacement for the original wood door, which had hung there for nearly a hundred years. All the windows were covered with heavy metal bars. The only way possible for them to escape was through the original, still operable, transom window over the door, which was too high for them to reach.

The only saving grace they had was the fact that the rapidly rising water was lifting them up to that window. Knowing they couldn't deal with the ice cold water very long, they maneuvered the huge, ancient, wood dining table from the dining room to the living room, and under the door. They tipped it upside down, and climbed on. As long as they didn't move the wrong way, the table floated stable enough to lift them until they reached the small window.

"What are we going to do after we get out," the younger, smaller of the girls asked. "The water's going to be awful cold."

"I know," the larger, older of the two answered. "But what choice do we have? We can't stay here. Even if we don't drown in here, what those guys are going to do to us will be worse when they come back."

"What could be worse than drowning?"

"Everything they're going to do to us. You haven't been here as long as I have, so you haven't seen the worst of it yet."

"Are you sure? Those guys raped me three times already."

"It would have been a lot more if it wasn't for the flood. They've done it to me, five or six of them at a time. More than once. It you're afraid of the water, you can stay. There's no way I am. No matter what the water out there is like."

"If you go, I'm going too. I just hope we live through it."

"So do I. But even if we don't, it's better than staying here and living the life they'll be forcing us into."

So they both went out the window. The bigger girl had to struggle hard to get through it, and had a few abrasions from the window frame by the time she did. The younger of the two easily slipped through the window.

The frigid cold of the water was enough to take away their breath when they landed in it, but they managed to keep their heads above it.

They were lucky at that point, and quickly found a log floating away from a would be future firewood pile. It was nearly six feet long, and large enough to allow both of them to climb on and straddle it. That left only their legs and feet still immersed in the deadly cold water.

They used their hands to slowly paddle away from the house. The older of the two girls was hoping against hope they would find some higher ground, where they could desert the log and walk to safety. Unfortunately, their luck wasn't going to hold out long enough for that to happen.

Instead of finding anything even close to high ground, they moved into St Catherine's current. Before they realized what was happening, the current had a tight hold on them. As they floated ever more rapidly down the river, it became increasingly difficult for them to hold on to the log.

After a short and wild ride, the log hit something else floating in the water. It spun around, throwing both of them into the water. They struggled to catch hold of their log, but failed to to do it. Still, they did all they could to stay afloat. The undertow from the uncontrolled current was too much.

The younger, smaller girl was the first to go under. She wasn't able to pull herself to the surface in time. The older of the two girls followed her under a short time later. As hard as they had tried to escape the prison they were forced into, they didn't quite make it.

CHAPTER 1

This particular bridge over the St. Catherine river was a long way from Deputy Sheriff Mack Thomas's favorite place. While the original version of it was being built, two young boys were murdered there. It was the place Mack was forced to kill a man. The first man he ever killed.

Several other people died when the original bridge collapsed. Among them was a dear friend of his wife's. And now Mack was standing in the middle of the bridge, looking at the wild rapids flowing closer to the bridges roadbed than he would have thought possible.

As he stood there, the only thing he could do is wonder if it was going to hold up to the raging torrent now running under it. Or would it collapse again? In truth, he personally didn't care. But because it was part of the county road system, he knew how much it would inconvenience a lot of people, so part of him hoped it would stay up through the beating it was taking.

He also wished that when the average person saw this flood, they would realize how the extremes of weather were constantly getting stronger and more destructive. Climate change, which was actually global warming, could be difficult to understand. So all too many people either didn't understand, or wouldn't accept that it was causing the new extremes.

It was apparently way too much to even hope for very much ever being done to curb the warming. Few people had any inclination to make the effort it takes to care about or work for the future. Not for the environment, and not for the long term fate of the human race. The pervasive attitude of most was simple. Grab what you can while you can. Life's too short to worry about anything more long term than yesterday.

Given the severe weather factor being caused by global warming, he knew that even if this bridge survived this onslaught, there'd be a future one to destroy it.

While he let his mind fill up with his depressing, doomsday thoughts, his eyes continued to watch the fast flowing water. They constantly moved from the water directly below him to the river upstream. A lot of debris was riding the rapids, but suddenly something caught his eyes. At first, he couldn't make out what the object was. Only that it was larger than most things he was seeing.

Then, as he focused on it, he felt his heart skip a beat as the shock of what it was hit him. The object was a human body. As it got closer, he realized it was a woman. Closer still, a young woman.

Even before it started its ride under the bridge, Mack was running down to the river bank, hoping to intercept it. It was too far out in the river for him to reach, so he followed it as it flowed down stream. There was a strong bend in the river about a half mile beyond the bridge, and there the river was piling all manner of debris, along with the body.

Mack still couldn't reach the body. But he used his cell phone to call for the support he needed to retrieve the body from the river, and to complete all the other tasks required with a discovery like this.

As always, there were a lot of questions asked as soon as support people began arriving. And, as always, the first question was, "How did you find the body here?" It was as if he should never of been there, that being there was doing something wrong.

He explained how he saw it in the river from above while he was on the bridge, and only followed it as it was taken by the river to this place. That of course brought on the questions wanting to know why he was on the bridge.

When the rescue squad from the local fire department arrived, Mack cut everyone's questions off, and explained to them how the body got there.

"Well," the man in charge of them said, "it shouldn't take too long to retrieve it."

As quickly as they got everything in place needed to get the job done, it should have been done quickly. The problem was, as soon as the lady working out in the river, at the end of a rope, was ready to connect a second rope to the body she stopped.

She shook her head, then yelled, "there's another one here. This one's buried in the debris, so it's going to take some effort to get it out."

Mack, along with most of the people who were there to assist in recovering the first body, groaned at the news. The news that there was a second body meant they'd all be there a lot longer than first anticipated. During the half of the year the Minnesota weather moderated, no one would have minded that much. Now though, it was early spring, which meant conditions often weren't much better than they were in the dead of winter.

It was already late afternoon, which meant dropping temperatures. Along with additional cold, the sky filled with dark clouds warned of coming snow.

As the tedious task of moving debris out of the way of the second body progressed, it became obvious that it would be dark before the body was recovered. So they brought in portable spot lights, often used at the scene of night time accidents, to assist in the recovery efforts.

It was late into the evening before the second body was pulled out of the river and removed from the sight. Snow had started an hour previous to that, and was now coming down hard.

By the time Mack reached home that night, his truck was in four wheel drive so he could keep moving. The wind driven snow drifts were sometimes as deep as three feet out on the rural county roads where he was.

He was shaking his head in disgust over the weather when he went into the house. What had started as just another heavy snow, was turning into a full scale blizzard.

His wife, Lisa, who was also a deputy sheriff, greeted him as he did. "That bad?" she said when she saw the look on his face.

"It's getting there," he told her. "It's blowing like the devil now, and the roads will be closed soon, if they aren't already."

"That tells us what tomorrow will be like, doesn't it?"

"Don't be surprised if we get called before morning. It's April. Not even people who live in Minnesota are ready for a blizzard in April."

"True," she agreed, "and just about everyone has put away their winter gear. Even the county. I'll bet they're working to get the snowplows back into service right now."

"Not much we can do about any of it though, other than wait and see. Have you eaten yet?"

"No, I was waiting for you."

"Okay, how about something simple tonight? Like maybe fried egg sandwiches?"

"Sounds good as anything. You fry the eggs and I'll make the toast and slice the tomatoes."

"We sure are lucky, aren't we, to have real tomatoes this time of the year."

"We are. Having these hot house tomatoes from your dad's greenhouse is always a treat this time of the year."

They no more than sat down to eat when the phone rang. It was the sheriff, Dale Magee. "We've got a head-on crash," he explained, "out on the four lane, about a mile south of Kingsburg. We could use some help, if you can make it."

"We'll try," Mack said, "but the roads out here are already drifted over bad. So I can't promise we can get through."

"Do your best. We really do need help with traffic control. Seems as though everyone's forgotten how to drive in the snow. We're constantly no more than a half step from another accident."

Mack and Lisa gobbled down their sandwiches, knowing it'd be best to eat while they could, with long night facing them. They dressed for the outside in light winter wear, and stashed heavier gear in the back of Mack's truck.

As soon as they turned onto the county road, they knew it was going to take quite a while to make it to the accident that Dale called them to help with. Even with four wheel drive and the extra weight Mack had in the back of the truck, movement was close to impossible.

It got even more complicated when they came to a small car in the ditch. Mack wanted to keep moving, knowing how difficult it would be to get moving again if he stopped. But he knew he couldn't, in good conscious, go by without checking on the car.

The drifts were already covering the car nearly halfway up its height, so he had to dig to open the door. He always carried a shovel with him, in the summer for mud and the winter for snow, so the effort to do it wasn't as bad as it otherwise would have been. When he opened the door, he found the body of a badly beaten young man.

He had obviously been there for a while. One of his hands was clinging to the steering wheel. In the other, he held a scrap of paper. A pen was laying on the seat next to him. Mack took the paper out of his hand. It was an envelope, holding a bill for a credit card.

Written on the back of the envelope with barely controlled hand writing was a short note. It said, 'they took Stacey. I tried to stop them…' The written line ended with a squiggly line that ran to the bottom of the envelope.

Mack looked again at the man, and realized he must have put up quite a struggle against whoever *they* were. He also knew that there wasn't much of anything he could do about what he'd found there, given the weather. Even if he could get the body out of the car and loaded onto his truck, it wouldn't solve anything. It would, in fact, disturb a crime scene. So he put the envelope with the note on it in his pocket and closed up the car.

"That took a while," Lisa said when he got back in his truck. "Didn't the people in the car want any help?"

"There was only one in the car, and he's dead." He told her what he'd found as he put his truck in gear and started to creep ahead again.

"Shouldn't we be doing something? It doesn't seem right, just leaving a dead body in a car and driving away."

"It isn't. But there isn't much we can do either," he explained. "He's dead and there's living folks who need our help. So that's what we're going to do first. We'll have to wait to take care of the man in the car."

"You're right, Mack, there really isn't anything we can do for him. It still doesn't seem right though."

"It's one of those things that won't seem right no matter what we do. But for me, it's the living who come first."

CHAPTER 2

The dim first light of morning greeted them as they moved the last of the temporary barriers they used for traffic control out of the way. Both cars from the head on collision were hauled off, and the last two wreckers were busy hauling careless drivers out of the snow filled ditches. The snow had finally abated, and traffic was moving near normal again.

For the first time since Mack and Lisa reached the accident site, they were talking to Sheriff Dale Magee. "And now you're telling me," he complained, "that we have to visit the scene of a probable homicide. One you two discovered, then deserted on your way here last night."

"There wasn't any choice, Dale," Mack told him. "We were in the middle of a blizzard, and you needed our help here."

"You could have called it in."

"Sure, and have the support staff get lost in a blizzard trying to get out there. You know as well as I do, none of their vehicles are equipped to deal with that kind of weather. As it is, we're going to need to get a snowplow on that road if we're going to get back there."

"I know. There wasn't much else you could have done. But I'm sure not in the mood for what we have to do now. It's been a long time since I can remember being this tired."

"I can't either, but we need to do what we need to do."

"It's not going to do any good to complain about it though," Lisa said. "No matter what, we are going to be real busy for quite a while. My gut says there's more to those two bodies that were pulled out of the river yesterday than simple drownings. If it would have been just one, I could maybe believe some kind of accident. But not two. Especially not two young girls. Young boys, maybe, they're often foolish enough to have that kid of accident. With girls, it's much less likely."

"It could be," Dale argued, "a case of one getting into trouble and one trying to save the other."

"It's possible, but I don't think so. I think there's a lot more to it than that."

"Time will tell I guess."

Dale made a phone call then. When he finished he said, "We can head out now. There'll be a plow on the road before we get there."

The car was difficult to see by the time they got to it. The blowing snow nearly covered it. Only part of the roof of it still showed. Mack took out his shovel and started digging right away. It wasn't until he managed to open the door that he remembered the envelope in his pocket. He gave it to Dale.

"So apparently someone took a person, probably female, named Stacey, and this person here was beaten to death trying to stop them."

"That's the way it looks."

"None of this is going to be fun. You know that, don't you Mack? And you, Lisa. What do you think about it all. Is being a deputy sheriff going to be what you thought it would be now that we're facing what we're facing."

She gave him a wry smile when she answered him. "What's the big deal, Dale," she asked. "All we just had was a blizzard. Only about a quarter of the county is under water. So far, we only have two very suspicious drownings. And finally, a homicide that was obviously committed somewhere other than the place we found the body. So what's the big deal?"

"When you put it that way, Lisa," Dale sighed heavily, "I guess not that much." But it was obvious that he felt like the weight of the world was on top of him.

Lisa and Mack stayed at the scene for another hour, then left for home. Dale told them, before they did, to get a few hours sleep before returning to work.

When they arrived home, it was still early enough to eat breakfast with the rest of their family. It had become a tradition over time, for them to gather, when possible, in the home of Mack's father Ben. He and his wife, Theresa, always made breakfast for anyone in the family, or even close friends, who showed up.

Since they all lived in close proximity, getting together wasn't at all difficult. They lived on a four hundred plus acre farm/ranch. Mack's father raised organic vegetables on forty acres of the land. The rest was either left in a natural wooded state, in pasture for their cattle, a special pasture just for their few horses, or hay fields. Mack's uncle Roy, along with his wife Wanda, were the primary people involved in taking care of the ranching part of the place during the warmer months. In the coldest part of winter, usually December through March, they spent their time in Texas. Roy and Wanda owned a small ranch there, which was run by a couple who lived on the place.

This morning they were all there, along with a good friend. Sue Sartor had become an unofficial member of the family in recent years. As often as possible, she ate breakfast with them. When she first started to join them for breakfast it wasn't on a regular basis because it was a long drive from where she lived.

That problem had been recently resolved however. She had done a lot for the family that they greatly appreciated. So they got together and set aside a five acre plot, and installed a new, two bedroom mobile home on it. They had it setup on a permanent foundation, so when it was done, it was much the same as a stick built house. They gave it to her as a present on her most recent birthday. That's why she was now considered and treated as if she actually was a part of the family.

When Mack and Lisa walked in for breakfast that morning, Roy, who always had a comment for them said, "You two look like you've been up all night. Did you have trouble sleeping?" he asked. Then he teased, "Or was it something else?"

Mack just shook his head and let Lisa answer him. "It was something else, Roy. Like finding a dead body in a car in the middle of the blizzard.

Directing traffic out on the four lane after a head on that killed three out of six people. Then finishing up the night with the dead guy in the car, as the forensic team analyzed the crime scene. Not to mention Mack was late getting home last night because he was helping to fish a couple of dead girls out of the river."

"I'm amazed you're here then," he said. "If it was me, I'd be dead on my ass and in bed already."

"We'd be there too," Mack said, "if we weren't as hungry as we are."

Nothing more had to be said about food. Ben and Theresa were already preparing their breakfast. They were both excellent cooks, so the quality of the food they served always rivaled that of the best breakfast cafes anywhere. It was also served in quantities to satisfy anyone's appetite. This morning was no exception. Along with the traditional food served at breakfast, there was also a plate of fresh, sliced tomatoes from Ben's greenhouse.

Eating to everyone's approval, Lisa ate a man-size meal. It was something she did on a regular basis, while still maintaining her near perfect figure.

"I sure wish I could do that," Sue said as Lisa finished eating. "How do you get away with eating the way you do? You never put on any weight. If I ate that much, I'd weigh three hundred pounds."

"I don't know," Lisa answered. "I've always eaten a lot. Even when I was a kid."

"It's her metabolism," Mack said. "Her's is faster than almost anyone else. But it's my guess, the day will come when she'll have to pay attention to how much she eats, the same of the rest of us."

His last comment made everyone laugh. "The same as the rest of us, Mack?" Wanda asked. "If anything, you pay less attention to how much you eat than even your wife."

"Yeah, well, my metabolism runs a little fast too."

They bantered back and forth on the subject for a few more minutes, until Roy changed the subject. "So what's the deal with the dead guy?" he asked.

Mack told them what he knew about the dead man, then about the envelope with the message. He ended it with, "There was a credit card bill inside the envelope. It was for the woman who was taken from the car. Dale's probably checked that out already."

"Do you have any ideas on why she was taken?"

"I'll answer that, Roy," Lisa told him, her voice hinting that there was some anger there. "I think it was done by human traffickers. There's been an extraordinary number of missing persons in this and surrounding states in recent months. Ninety percent of them female, with the same percentage of females being under twenty-five."

"That sure sounds like a definite problem. What's being done about it?"

"Not near enough, Roy. Not anywhere near enough. We're doing what we can, but we're confined to our county. We need the state police to step in. And actually, the FBI should be looking into it too."

"Why aren't they?"

Lisa nearly laughed at the question, but managed to contain herself. "That, Roy, is something you already know the answer too. We now have a Republican governor and the Republicans are in control of the house and senate. And the president is avoiding the issue."

"Yeah, I see your point. But if it was girls missing from cities in the east, then there'd be something done. Especially if any of them came from prominent conservative families."

"That's right, Roy, but what's happening here isn't near so important. We're fly over land. Not important. Look at what the FBI has done about the untold numbers of missing Native American women over the past several years. Almost nothing. So we're going to get very little help here. If the governor was still a Democrat, we'd at least have the state police looking into it."

"What about the two girls who drowned. Do you know anything about them?"

This time Mack answered. "Not much. Most of us think it was just a tragic accident of some kind. I doubt though, that we'll ever know for sure what happened."

"You said most of you think it was an accident. Who doesn't?"

"Guess."

Roy looked at Lisa, who now had a grim look on her face. "Why don't you think it was an accident?" he asked her.

"Actually, I don't have a solid opinion yet, either way. It's possible it was an accident. But before I can accept that, there's too many unanswered questions."

"What kind of questions?"

"Where are the girls from. Why were they near the river. How did they end up in the water. Why were they even outside on such a miserable day."

Mack's cell phone rang then. The room was silent until his conversation ended. "That was Dale," he said. "The dead guy in the car was a Calvin Sword. He was engaged to the missing women, who was only eighteen. She was Stacey Baker. They lived in Minneapolis and were on their way to St Cloud. We still don't have any idea where they were attacked."

"Did he tell you anything about the girls?" Lisa asked.

Mack shook his head yes, then met her eyes. "I think you were born to be in law enforcement," he told her. "And I'm beginning to believe that your talents are being wasted here. You should be an FBI agent, or in some really important place."

"Why would you say that, Mack?"

"Those girls. You were right in not believing their drowning was just an accident. The drowning itself could have been, but they've been missing for more than a week now. They were last seen in a mall in Minnetonka."

"I think you're right, Mack," Roy said. "She sure does have the instincts for the work."

"No more than Mack does," Lisa argued. "What I have, is a special interest in crimes like those we're now involved in. And you all know why that is."

And they did. She was kidnapped and raped when she was a teenager, and still had a strong hatred for men who were guilty of those crimes. No one in that family had any negative feelings about her because of it.

Knowing then what Lisa's mood was when they went home, Mack made it a point to avoid any physical contact when they got there. She showered first, and was in bed before he finished his. Believing she was asleep, he was careful not to disturb her when he literally crawled into bed.

She surprised him then, when she quickly moved over him. She wasn't wearing pajamas. "I hate those men, Mack," she said. "But I love you, and I'm thankful that we have between us what we have." She then used her hand to guide him.

He reacted to her reaction to him the only way he could, which included a satisfied smile. As he always did when situations like this involved the two of them, he marveled at her ability to separate her love for him, and the near deadly emotions she felt toward the men who constantly hurt women.

CHAPTER 3

Sheriff Tod Mcintire was disgusted. Standing in several inches of water, he stared at the open transom window over the steel door he had installed. It should have been enough to temporarily hold the girls. It was only three days ago that he'd locked them in this house. He knew how stupid he'd been for not doing anything about the window. But it had not occurred to him that they'd find a way to reach high enough to crawl out of it.

Now they were gone, and according to the news, they'd drowned in the river. Normally, it wasn't that much of a river any longer. At one time, it was of a respectful size, but with all the recent irrigation being done, it had shrunk considerably. Until the spring flood anyway. Now it rivaled what the Mississippi was during a normal flow. It now carried enough water to flood most of the low ground in Jackstone county, the kind of location where house they were in was located.

"Trouble was," Sheriff Mcintire decided, "nothing was normal now." He spent a lot of money to build the underground bunker where he kept the girls before they were shipped out east, but with things the way they were, it was now full of water. If it wasn't, the two girls would never have been left in the house to start with.

His thoughts were interrupted then, by a howl from a bedroom located in the upper level of the house. He was not at all in the mood to listen to that kind of noise. Especially when it came from someone who was scheduled to be shipped with the next bunch of girls.

"Please," the woman cried, "don't hurt my baby."

The sheriff walked into the room and up to the bed. He threw the big man, struggling to rape the young woman under him, onto the floor.

"You've been told to keep your hands off the merchandize," he growled. "Now get the hell out of here."

He turned to the woman. "Please," she pleaded, "Don't let them hurt my baby. Hurt me if you have to, but please, not the baby."

"You're pregnant?"

"Yes."

"How far along?"

"About two and a half months."

He thought about her answer. He could pretend he didn't know about it, and ship her even though pregnant females were among the last thing his customers wanted.

He thought about using her locally for a while, but decided that he'd be pushing his luck too far if he did that. Her picture had already been flashed all over the news, with a reward of ten thousand dollars offered for her rescue or return. Going for that was tempting, but he knew it was too risky to try. That left only one option.

Before he used it, he decided to use her. She was very pretty, with a nice figure and fairly large breasts. He told her as he started to undress. "It's like this," he explained, keeping a friendly tone to his voice. "I do not want to do anything that could possibly hurt your baby. But to be sure that I don't, you have to cooperate with me. You can't be fighting me when I take off your clothes. Not when I do what I'm going to do either. In fact, if you work with me, you might find yourself liking it."

Stacey Baker was so filled with concern for the baby she carried inside her, that she decided to let this man do whatever he was going to do to her. It was all she could do to not gag when he moved over her and forced himself on her, but with all her will, she managed to avoid struggling with him.

She felt an immense relief when he finally finished with her. It was short lived. He quickly moved his hands around her neck and squeezed. Now she did struggle with everything she had to struggle with. It was to no avail. His hands held her tight until she went limp, and death owned her.

He dressed, called the man he'd thrown out of the room, and the two of them carried her outside and dumped her into the back of an old pickup. "Take her to the river and get rid her," he ordered.

Why should I have to do it. You killed her."

"You have to do it because I told you that you have too."

"It still ain't fair."

"Fair is the fact that I haven't gotten tired enough of your sorry ass to kill you yet. So don't make me so tired that you're the next one they find floating in that damn river."

Knowing the sheriff wasn't kidding, the man got in the pickup and drove to the river.

CHAPTER 4

Mack woke up early, feeling tense and edgy. He eased himself out of bed, not wanting to disturb Lisa. After using the bathroom he went directly to the kitchen and the coffee pot. Instead of a modern, automatic coffee maker, he used an old fashion porcelain percolator. It was the same kind as his father, Ben, used. It produced a beverage with a richer flavor, and the aroma from the percolating coffee was something that couldn't be created any other way.

As quiet as he tried to be while he put the pot together, the sound of it woke Lisa anyway. She joined him in the kitchen wearing a flannel bath robe, which was held closed by a simple tie.

After a quick look at her, Mack said, "That robe you're wearing is trying hard to hide most of you, but it isn't working. It's only making my imagination work full time."

She tipped her head to one side, smiled, then said, "I think you're remembering more than imagining, Mack. Either way though, I'm glad you still notice."

"That's something I'll never stop doing. There's nothing in the world that makes me take notice more than you do."

She kissed him on the cheek. "That's a nice thing to say. Now pour me a cup of that coffee. It smells delicious."

He poured her a cup, then told her, "I'm sorry I woke you up. I was trying not too."

"Don't worry about it. You are only partially responsible for my being up now. I've been off and on waking up all night. After all that happened yesterday, my mind's been full of questions."

"Mine too," Mack agreed. "That's why I got up so early. I think I'll skip breakfast this morning, and get out and about early. Even if I don't accomplish anything relevant."

"Me too."

Lisa was still dressing when Mack left. He was anxious to get out, but not sure what to do first. So he did what he frequently did when his mind was full of questions without any good answers. He drove the newly plowed roads to the wildlife refuge. What he saw when he got there shocked him, even though he knew better than to expect anything else.

The refuge was less than half the size it was just a few years ago. The federal government sold a large portion of it for a huge resort complex which included apartments, condos, townhouses, a shopping mall, and of course, two eighteen hole golf courses.

Eventually, because the Republicans hated it, the remaining refuge was put up for sale. They wanted it to go to someone who would turn it into some commercial project or another. Instead, it was purchased by a group determined to keep it as a wildlife refuge, rather than be developed.

It continued to serve as a refuge for all native life forms in the area until tragedy struck. After a prolonged drought, the entire refuge burned in a disastrous wild fire.

As nature does when left alone with its own devices, recovery started quickly and continued steadily. But now, with it covered by a new, deep snowfall, the only lifeforms showing were the still standing tree trunks. And nearly all of them were dead, charred from the fire. All of it together produced the image of a deserted, bombed out battlefield.

If he hadn't been watching the steady recovery of the refuge during the warm months, the scene would have been devastating for Mack. But because he had been watching it closely, the horrifying sight only served to remind him of the stupidity of the humans who allowed so much of the refuge to be totally destroyed when the resort was built.

With that thought in mind, he decided to stop at the bridge where he spotted the body of one of the girls recovered yesterday. Before driving up on the bridge, he drove passed the spot where the two bodies were recovered. He didn't get far before he slammed on the brakes and stared. He couldn't believe what he was seeing.

Tangled in the ever growing piles of debris was another body. Filled with the sense of the unreal, he used his cell phone to call the support people needed to deal with this situation.

The first to arrive was Sheriff Dale Magee. "You sure do know how to interrupt a happy marriage, don't you, Mack," he complained. "Right now, my wife is anything but happy with you. Even with another body in the water, she thinks you should have waited a while to call. I'm close to thinking the same thing. So what the hell are you doing out here at this hour, Mack?"

"Next time," Mack snapped back, "turn off your cell phone. We turn them both off at appropriate times." He stopped talking just long enough so his words would let Dale know he didn't need to be jumped on for doing his job. "I'm out here this early because of all that happened yesterday. It's bugging me. And now," he pointed out in the river where the rescue workers were working to recover the body, "I'm wondering even more about what's going on."

"We're all thinking and worrying about it. But none of us started our day hours early because of it."

"I know, but maybe it's time everyone put forth full effort to solve this problem. Four bodies in two days. I'd say the problem is now too serious to be taken any other way. We've got to do more than we've been doing."

"I won't argue that with you, Mack. But we are limited. Our jurisdiction stops at the county borders."

"Why does it have too?"

"Because that's the way the system works. I'm called a *county* sheriff for a reason."

"I know all that. But whatever the rules are, if following those, or any rules to the letter costs people their lives, maybe it's time to bend them a little."

"Okay, Mack. What is it you have on your mind this time?"

"Nothing right now. But after the weather changes back to more or less normal, and fishing opens up again, I think Paul and I should do some fishing a ways north of here."

"You wouldn't be thinking of Jackstone county, now would you?"

"I would. It's only a short distance upstream from here, and you know as well as I do, there's been issues with this kind of activity up there in the past."

"If you do that, I'll need to inform Tod Mcintire about what you're doing."

"That wouldn't be a good idea."

"Why not. He's the sheriff there. It's the right thing to do. We owe him that courtesy."

"Actually, we don't. Not after the way he treated Lisa." Mack referred to an incident Lisa was involved in when she was kidnapped and successfully defended herself and escaped. Sheriff Mcintire accused her of murder. "Not to mention, doing that will totally defeat the purpose of our going up there."

"I know you don't like him, Mack, but he admitted he was wrong about Lisa."

"Only because he didn't have a choice. I think we have to treat him as a suspect. I'm not totally sure about him either way, but Lisa's convinced he's guilty of human trafficking. She's positive he's involved in it in a big way."

"The trouble with that is, Mack, she doesn't have any positive proof."

"As far as I'm concerned, when she has a gut reaction as strong as this one is, that's proof enough for me."

"I'm inclined to agree with you. The trouble is I'm obligated, by law, to work with him on crimes like this."

"Well, I understand how it is for you, Dale. So I'll forget about trying to check out the activity up there. We'll just have to do the best we can do here, and let it go at that."

"I didn't ask you to do that. I think your idea is a good one. I only think we need to notify the sheriff of what you're doing."

Mack just shook his head and redirected his attention to the recovery efforts going on out in the river. The debris that was in the way was removed, and the rescue crew was attaching ropes to the body needed to lift it out of the water.

When they got it into the boat and the boat to shore, Mack and Dale checked the body. It was Stacey Baker, the woman who was abducted from the car Calvin Sword was found in. They'd seen her picture on her driver's license, and as bad as it was, it was still accurate enough to identify her.

The bruising on her neck was all they needed to tell them the cause of death.

"I wonder why she was murdered?" Mack said. "She's young enough, and certainly good looking enough, to have been sold into their sex slavery ring. As were the two girls taken out of the river yesterday. I don't know why this one was murdered, but I think the weather had something to do with the other two. Somehow, the flood created a situation that allowed them to escape. It's too bad they didn't make it."

"Given how little evidence we have on any of this, Mack, you're drifting a long way out there."

"I know," he agreed. "We've been there, done that before." He bowed his head, shaking it slowly, his face showing his feeling of futility. "Even so, it's too damn bad we won't be doing anything to check it out."

Seeing the discouraged look on Mack's face was the last thing Dale wanted. "We might not be able to deal with this exactly the way you want to, Mack, but we will for sure be doing everything we can."

"Maybe, but we'll be doing it awful slow. How many women will end up forced to be slave prostitutes, or murdered, in the meantime?"

"I don't know. Even one is too many. So like you, I wish we could do more."

"Then let's do more."

CHAPTER 5

They'd spent a fun night shopping and weren't paying much attention to their surroundings when they left the mall. It was crowded with cars and massive piles of snow when they got there. So their car was parked in the outer reaches of the huge parking lot that went around the entire mall.

Neither one of the girls noticed the twenty-four foot C-class RV until it was close behind them. As they turned to see what was making the noise, two men quickly left it. As fast as the girls started to scream, the men grabbed them and forced them inside. The RV quickly accelerated, leaving the parking lot for the freeway. It traveled west until it reached a four lane which would take them north.

The men inside the camper were each holding one of the girls in their lap, waiting to get further north and out of the main stream traffic before they tried to tie them up. They did, however, use the time to run their hands over the girl's bodies.

They were just inside Clayborne county when they decided to tie them. Both girls were terrified, but fought back fiercely when the men attempted it. They fought hard enough to actually rock the camper back and forth slightly.

Behind them, a deputy sheriff noticed the motion of the vehicle. She didn't stop it, but did radio the license plate to check on it. When it came back as stolen, she turned on her lights to pull it over. She again used her radio to report the stop, her location, and a request for backup.

She waited for it to arrive, then cautiously left her car to approach the camper on the driver's side. The backup deputy moved up on the camper from the other side. Suddenly there was a scream from inside the camper and the driver pulled a weapon.

A second scream rang out, and the driver panicked. He pointed the gun he'd been holding at the deputy, who was almost to his door, and shot her in the chest twice. Then he slammed the camper in gear and drove away with the accelerator on the floor.

Rather than give chase, the deputy who was on the right side of the camper, immediately checked on the condition of the deputy on the ground. She was wearing body armor, so she was still alive. But the gun that shot her was a powerful one. It not only knocked her down, but took the wind out of her. Along with that, she was destined to have two huge bruises on her chest.

Her backup was taking no chances, and called an ambulance for her. He also called for more backup to check out the shooting scene and do something with her car.

Because it was one of his deputies who was shot, Sheriff Dale Magee was also called. After he checked out the scene, interviewed the deputy still there, and drove to the hospital to check on the deputy who was shot, he made one phone call.

Mack answered his cell phone on the fifth ring. "It must be bad," his groggy voice said, "if you're calling me this late, Dale."

"It could be worse," Dale told him, then asked Mack to come into the office when he went on duty. I'll explain what happened tonight when you and Lisa get here in the morning. I only called now because we do need to have a meeting first thing. Paul will be here too. He had planned on taking the day off."

"Are you sure you don't need me to come in now?" Mack asked.

"Morning will be good enough. We'll talk then." Dale hung up.

A very sleepy Lisa turned over then. "What did Dale want?" she asked, without having to ask who called. If Mack got a call late, or in the middle of the night, the odds were huge that it would be work and Dale doing the calling.

"Something happened tonight that he didn't want to take the time to explain right now. And he wants me to go into the office first thing, along with you, for a meeting. Whatever it is, for him to call me now, it's got to be serious."

"I'm sure it is," she said. "And that's all the more reason to try and get some sleep. Come back to bed."

He did, and she curled her back up against him. She took his hand and placed it over her bare breast, then promptly fell asleep. When morning came, they hadn't moved from that position. Realizing that, Mack wasn't sure he wanted to leave the bed. Not for a while anyway.

Lisa definitely didn't want to, but remembered the late night phone call. "I hate to do this to us," she said, "but we have to get up. We have a meeting with Dale, so we really shouldn't be late."

Reluctantly, Mack agreed, and got out of bed. They had enough time to get ready and still eat a quick breakfast with the family. Roy asked them his favorite question when they got there.

"So what are the plans for today, guys?"

"We don't know," Lisa answered. "Dale called last night, and we're having some sort of meeting first thing."

"He didn't tell you why?"

"No, he had too many other things left to do when he called. Said he would explain this morning."

"Do you think," Roy asked, "that it might be about those two girls who were kidnapped last night? It's been all over the news this morning."

"We haven't listened to the news yet," Mack said. "What should we know about two girls being kidnapped?"

"They were taken at the mall…" Roy went on to tell them what happened, and that someone had seen it. That's why there weren't the usual doubts by the police that it actually did happen.

"It's possible that it has something to do with what our meeting is about, but I'm not at all sure how it would. I guess we'll learn that at the meeting."

They ate their, as always, delicious breakfast, then left for Dale's meeting. Mack followed Lisa into town, and parked on the street behind her when they got there. The office parking lot was already full, because a good portion of the sheriff's staff was there. And, a fair amount of the lot was filled with piles of snow.

"Good," Dale said as soon as they walked in, "you're here. Now we can start the meeting." Dale waved for them to move up to the front of the group standing there.

They'd arrived ten minutes early, but were the last to arrive anyway. Mack wasn't surprised by that, but he was surprised by the number of people involved in the meeting.

"I'm sure," Dale said to start things off, "most of you have seen the lead story today. Two girls were kidnapped last night…" he went on to tell them about that, then explained about the deputy who made the traffic stop. "And because of the eye witness, we know they were forced into a RV when they were taken. We're sure it was the same one the deputy stopped."

"How is she doing," Mack asked Dale.

"From what I've been told, she's got a couple of serious bruises, but the body armor she was wearing stopped both bullets. Luckily, she doesn't have any cracked or broken ribs. She'll be getting out of the hospital today. She'll be taking a couple of days off, but then she'll be back to work."

Someone made the comment, "She sure was lucky she was wearing her armor. It sounds like she wouldn't have made it if she wasn't."

Dale raised his voice when he answered the comment. "She wasn't lucky. She was *smart!* Uncomfortable or not, wearing armor just makes sense. Not wearing it makes no sense, and can prove to be stupid. Remember that on those days you're tempted to take it off."

Dale concluded the meeting with new instructions on how to deal with suspicious vehicles, and with a warning to be especially cautious on all future traffic stops. Everyone was also told to call for backup if there was anything questionable about the persons or vehicle being stopped.

As he ended the meeting, he asked detective Paul Danielson, along with Mack and Lisa, to stay.

"We have to discuss your idea about some undercover work in other counties," Dale said. "Now that this human trafficking problem has hit us directly, I feel like we're justified in moving ahead with our own investigation."

"I definitely agree," Mack said. "But if it involves any of the three of us doing any undercover work after Sheriff Tod Mcintire is informed about what we're doing, I'll strenuously object. And if it's Lisa doing it… well, it better not be Lisa doing it. Not under those circumstances."

"It won't be, Mack. If she's involved, it'll be done your way."

"I think that's wise," Paul interrupted. "I've been doing some checking on Sheriff Mcintire, and his past is shaky. He once was a cop in Madison Wisconsin. He was asked to resign because of some inappropriate behavior with a young girls. I think we'd be pushing it to trust him."

"I agree with Mack and Paul," Lisa said. "Trusting him won't simply be stupid, it'll make anything we're trying to do in his county extremely dangerous. Personally, I have no doubts at all that he's very much involved in most, if not all, human trafficking happening in the five state area."

Dale was a bit surprised by the strength of her words. "It sounds like you're sure he's guilty, Lisa. Do you have any proof to back up your beliefs?"

"If you mean hard core evidence, no, I don't. But when you've been through what I have, you develop a sixth sense about his kind of crimes, and the men who commit them. He's guilty, and it's up to us to prove it."

Dale looked at Mack and Paul. "Well, do you agree with her."

"I do," Mack answered without the slightest hesitation.

Paul's answer was slower. He scratched his head, then looked up at the ceiling as he formulated his answer. "I've been at this for a long time, and it's been my experience that victims often think they know something, when all it is, is their emotions overriding their common sense. But I also know that sometimes people do have the sixth sense that Lisa says she has. In this case, I have no doubt at all that she has it. So I most definitely do agree with her. More than that, I think you should consider giving her the lead in this case. She has a better feel for what they're doing, than any of us will ever have."

At that, Dale knew his deputies were right. Lisa was given the lead.

CHAPTER 6

As often happens in Minnesota, the weather became perverse. Two days after the April blizzard, the temperature reached seventy degrees. It continued warm for days. The fast melt that followed increased the flooding beyond anyone's expectations. Damage caused by the additional flooding was also beyond what was normal for spring flooding. Several bridges were washed out. All of the bridges in Clayborne County that were under water or washed out were in rural areas, but the bridge that left a bad taste in Mack's mouth managed to hold.

For more than a week, people throughout the state were forced to take detours just to get to work. Even in places that had never before flooded were under water. At least for a short time.

Sand bagging was used where possible, but even with a few thousand volunteers working at filling them, it was impossible to provide all that were needed. Somehow though, if a bank in a small town was in danger of being flooded, it was quickly surrounded with sand bags.

In the refuge several of the water control structures were damaged. Some needed replacement, but most were found repairable once the flood waters receded.

Most people from the sheriff's office volunteered their spare hours to the sand bag effort. Mack and Lisa, along with the rest of the Thomas family, were among them. But when the flooding abated, Mack gave his free hours to the vast amount of work that needed to be done in the refuge. The work moved along fairly smoothly for the first few days, until a few gun happy men started appearing.

The first incident happened on an early Saturday morning. Mack started at first light that morning to make some repairs on a foot bridge over a small creek, which was damaged by the flood. He wanted to get it done, so the trail it serviced could be opened in the near future.

He'd just started cutting a two by six with a hand saw, to be used for the top of a hand rail, when he heard the gun shot. It was followed by several more. It came from the far side of a hill north of where he was working. Without hesitation, he stopped what he was doing and drove his pickup in the direction of the gunshots.

Because the refuge was so open since the fire, he quickly found three young men working on the carcass of a yearling doe. They ignored him as he drove up.

"You know, don't you," he said, "that it's a long way to deer season?"

"So what," the biggest of the three answered. "This is a private refuge, and my dad's company is the major owner of it. He said we can hunt here. That means we can hunt here. You don't like it, you know what part of me you can kiss."

That was enough for Mack. Given all the problems he needed to deal with, a smart-ass poacher wasn't one he was about to tolerate. "I could use the standard line," he told the person who'd just told him a lie, "and say I hate to tell you this. That would be a lie though. Because I'm more than happy to tell you this. You are under arrest for poaching. You broke a state law when you did that. You are also under arrest for trespassing. There's an ordinance in Clayborne County against carrying a firearm on private land without permission. One more thing. You are under arrest for bringing a firearm into this refuge. According to our charter, no one is allowed to bring a firearm in here without a special permit."

"You can't arrest us. You ain't nobody."

"I don't have to be anybody, other than a citizen of this country. So, yea I can arrest you." Mack took out his cell phone and hit speed dial. When someone answered at the other end, he said, "Mack Thomas, requesting backup…" he went on to give his location and the reason for the request.

In minutes his backup arrived as a pair. Two deputies who were relatively close when the call went out responded to it. They were both smiling when they got out of their cars.

The first deputy couldn't resist making a comment. "These the creeps?" he asked.

"They are. This one here claims he can shoot all the deer he wants to in this refuge. Says his daddy's company owns most of it."

"He's certainly full of it, isn't he. What do you want to do with them?"

"I want you to make note of all the violations of the law, no matter how minor, and when you get them to the office, charge them with each and every one of them. Then lock them up. I also want you to take the big one in separate from the other two, and keep them separated after they're booked. I've got some tools over by my truck I was using to repair a foot bridge when they started shooting. As soon as I get them picked up, I'll join you at the office."

As he walked to his truck, he made the call to have the deer carcass picked up, then called Lisa to tell her he'd be later getting home than expected.

When he got to the station, he was met by the father of the biggest of the three poachers. Mack could easily tell from the father's stance and look on his face that he was angry. He purposely ignored him. That made the father irate.

"I don't know who the hell you think you are," the father yelled, "but you're screwing with the wrong person, locking up my son the way you did."

"I'm just a deputy sheriff doing his job. Who the hell are you that I'm supposed to be afraid of you?"

"I happen to be an executive vice president at the Lands Magnificent Corporation, and it happens to own that refuge. They have given full permission for my son to hunt there."

Mack looked at him, frowned, and said, "You are full of shit. I've been doing battle with your company for years. It owns the resort, and made a relatively small contribution when the rest of the refuge was sold to its current owners. In no way does it actually own any of it. The whole thing is run under a special trust by a board of directors. So save your bullshit for one of the many, waste of time, meetings I'm sure you'll be attending in the future."

"It's not me who's full of it. Once I tell Rodney Twillabee about this, he'll have the full weight and force of the corporation on you. The first thing he'll do is have your job. Then…"

Mack couldn't help it. His job had been threatened so many times by so many people that it had become a standing joke. He burst out laughing. The threat was always ridiculous, but coming from this guy, it was doubly so.

"If I were you," Mack said when he finally stopped laughing, "I'd stop the threats while you still can. When Rodney calls me, you can bet I'll mention all of them to him. If there are enough of them to irritate him, it could well be that it'll be your job that's in jeopardy."

"You can't laugh at me like that. You can't threaten me either. I can tell that you think you can do as you please because you wear a badge, but this time you are in serious trouble."

Mack knew that any further contact with the man was a waste of time, and just walked away from him. He sat down at his desk to do the paper work required to complete the arrest of the three men. He was near the end of it when Twilabee called.

"Sorry about the trouble, Mack," he said. "I've informed that obnoxious VP that he's no longer a VP, and that he's to shut his mouth, pay whatever fines there are, regardless of the amount. I also told him to keep his trouble making son the complete hell out of the refuge."

"Thanks, Rodney," Mack answered. "I appreciate it."

"No problem. Take care now."

Before the three men were released, Mack and the local game warden confiscated the truck they were using that day. It was only three months old and had a sticker price at the top end when it was sold. They also confiscated the three rifles they were using. All of them were high priced weapons. When they went to court, the judge fined each of them several thousand dollars for poaching and firearms violations.

When the three poachers were leaving the courtroom that day, Mack stopped them. "I hope," he said, "that this incident teaches you all something. That refuge is a place set aside for animals who no longer have anyplace else to live. It definitely is not a place for idle little rich boys to play."

The idle little rich boys walked away from him without answering. Mack was sure, before he said anything to them, that it was an exercise in futility, but he had to try.

Just as he was sure that nothing he did was going to change much in life for the better, he had to do the best he could. At least, for his small part of the world.

CHAPTER 7

From the time the deputy was shot, everyone in Clayborne County's sheriff's department paid close attention to all RVs, regardless of size. The traffic stops were far more frequent than normal but, if anything, fewer tickets for traffic violations were handed out.

Occasionally, a stop proved to be beneficial. Lisa pulled over a thirty-two foot class A one morning. It was driving erratically, drifting from one lane to another. When it stopped at the side of the road, she approached it with caution.

The elderly driver slurred his words, and otherwise appeared to be under the influence of either drugs or alcohol. Because of the ongoing need for extra caution, she called for backup, which arrived in minutes. She then told the driver to step out of the vehicle.

He ignored her, and continued to sit there with his head rolling around and his hands clutching the steering wheel. She again asked him to step out, and this time an older woman climbed over the man and stuck her head out the window.

"He can't come out," she said. "He's diabetic and I think he's having an insulin reaction. He needs to eat something with sugar in it, but I don't have any candy. Do you have anything?"

Lisa didn't, but they were in a RV. It was unlikely that anyone traveling in one wouldn't have something sweet along with them. She hurried inside and the first place she checked was the refrigerator. She didn't have to look hard to find a half gallon bottle of orange juice. It was, Lisa knew, one of the best, and quickest reacting things she could give him. She poured a glass, then fed it to the driver. She started with small sips, then as the sugar in the juice entered his system and started to counter the affects of the insulin, she gave him bigger drinks.

By the time he finished the glass, he was recovered enough to drink on his own. The lady inside the RV, who apparently was the driver's wife, was ready to leave.

Lisa wasn't about to let them go under these circumstances. Instead, she asked the woman, "Why didn't you help him yourself? Don't you know what to do when someone has an insulin reaction?"

"I certainly do. You give them candy. That's what I always do. I just forgot to bring any along this time."

"Candy isn't the only thing with sugar in it. You probably have a dozen or more things that would have worked."

"Well, how am I supposed to know that?"

"By learning how to deal with diabetes. How long has your husband been diabetic?"

"His doctor diagnosed it about a year ago. He said to give him candy when something like this happens?"

"Is that all he told you?"

"Well, no. He told us a lot of stuff, but I don't remember much of it."

"What about your husband? Doesn't he remember?"

"You don't have to talk about me like I'm not here," the husband interrupted. "And no, I don't remember much of what the doctor said. That's her job." He pointed at his wife. "I'm the one who provides our income. So it's up to her to do the rest."

"Since neither one of you seems to have even a basic understanding of the problem you have, I can't allow you to go any farther in this vehicle."

"What are we supposed to do? How can we go up north if you won't let us go in our RV?"

"You'll have to find another way to travel. Preferably home, where you can spend your free time learning about diabetes and how to handle things like insulin reactions. You don't, and sooner or later, one of them could kill him."

"Well," she complained, "I think you're making too big an issue out of this. It's not like we had an accident or something."

"Given the condition he was in when I stopped you, you wouldn't have gotten much farther without one."

Lisa ended the discussion there. She wrote them a ticket, asked the backup deputy to give the couple a ride to the station where they could use their cell phone to call someone to help them. She stayed with the RV until it was towed away.

She was finally ready to be on her way, when another RV, this one a class C, drove by her. It was moving under the speed limit, but something was causing it to rock back and forth. Since there was no apparent reason for it to be doing that, she immediately became suspicious.

She drove onto the four lane with three cars and a pickup between her and the RV. The rocking that caught her attention continued until it swerved from the right lane into the left, then back to the right lane. She knew then that it was time to stop it. She turned on her lights, but instead of stopping, the RV accelerated.

Lisa moved up behind it, then used her radio to request that anyone who might be on or near the four lane north of Kingsburg to watch for the RV. She also requested that they, if at all possible, stop the vehicle.

Unfortunately, there were no deputies patrolling in that area at that time, so she requested backup. Something she knew she wouldn't have for a while. In order to back her up, someone would have to travel at a very high speed to catch up with her.

She continued to follow until the county line, then crossed it. She was sure, given the speed the RV was traveling, it was trying to dodge more than a traffic ticket. The chase continued through the second county, then moved into the third county. Sheriff Tod Mcintire's Jackstone county.

Less than two miles into the county a sheriff's car pulled out onto the highway in front of her. It pleased her to see she had backup. It was short lived. A second sheriff's car moved in behind her. They both turned on their lights and slowed down. She had no choice but to pull over to the side of the road.

She was more than a little angry when she got out of her pickup. "What in the hell do you guys think you're doing?" she asked. "I've been chasing that RV since Kingsburg."

"We don't know nothing about that," one of the sheriff's deputies said. "All we know is that you're tearing through our county at an extremely high rate of speed. So now you're under arrest for speeding, reckless and careless driving, and resisting arrest."

They cuffed her, loaded her in the back of one of their cars, and took her to the sheriff's office. What they didn't realize, was the fact that the Clayborne County deputy who had been trying to catch up with Liza the whole time, witnessed what they were doing. He immediately called Dale on his cell phone and told him what happened.

Since Dale knew what Sheriff Tod Mcintire had tried to do to Lisa during a previous incident, he didn't waste any time. He called Mack, Paul, and three other deputies. The other three were the biggest of all the deputies in the department.

They left in two vehicles. Mack drove his pickup, with Paul riding shotgun. Dale and the other three rode in the sheriff's car. With sirens wailing, they drove at top speed. When they arrived at Tod Mcintire's office, they didn't fool around. They walked in with guns drawn. There were only four men men in the office. Two of them were in a cell with Lisa. They were trying, rather unsuccessfully, to strip her blouse off.

Mack moved into the cell and slammed his pistol onto the back of the head of one of the men there. He dropped to the floor. That allowed Lisa to deal with the second one. She slammed her fingers into his eyes, blinding him. Then she pushed him just far enough to give him a solid kick between the legs. When he doubled over she gave him a second kick, which landed under his chin. His neck made an audible snap when his head flew back.

She wasn't finished though. She walked up to the sheriff. "Now," she said, her voice telling him she meant it. "It's me and you. You can fight back or not, but I'm going to make you wish you'd never heard of me."

"You talk tough, when your friends all have guns on me."

Lisa turned to them. "Let him fight. If he wins, let him go."

The sheriff watched Dale and the rest of them holster their weapons. He was sure he'd have no trouble beating Lisa in any kind of a fight, and knew from the looks he was getting that a fight with her was the only chance he had.

Without warning, he took his best swing at her. With most people, the fight would have ended there. Lisa wasn't most people. She expected a move like that from him. He was, at heart, little more than a backyard bully, and would use every dirty tactic he could think of to defeat her. His problem was, she knew everyone of them too. She just didn't need them as bad as he did.

She countered his wild swing with the palm of her right hand landing hard on his nose. She could hear as well as feel the satisfying crunch. There was nothing like a little blood to get a fight started. He was still sure he'd beat her, and he took a boxer's stance.

She smiled at him. He was doing a good job of covering his face and upper body, but that left his legs open for her. He might think he was in a boxing match now, but she was in a fight. And it was a fight she wanted to win as bad as she'd ever want to win one.

His anger at her constant smile was growing in him. Who the hell did she think she was, smiling at him. He moved in on her fast, trying to pump both hands into her stomach. This left his head open again, so as she sidestepped him, she landed a heavy blow to his temple with the side of her fist. It staggered him enough to allow her to move slightly behind him. She slammed her foot into the back of his knee. As it folded, she kicked again, this time between his legs from behind.

The blow was painful enough for him to momentarily reach for the spot with both hands. she quickly moved around in front of him and landed a barrage of blows into his stomach, then even more on his face. On his way down, she gave him the same kick under his chin she gave the first deputy she fought.

The sheriff was still conscious, so Lisa knelt down and moved close to his ear, "You ever try to do anything to me again, you son of a bitch, and you have my solemn promise that I will kill you."

With the sheriff laying there, bruised and beaten, she stood. She didn't have a scratch on her.

It was now Mack's turn to talk. A talk he aimed at Sheriff Tod Mcintire. "It's like this, Asshole, the beating she gave you is just a start. Come tomorrow, you and your entire department are going to find out what lawyers can do to people who do what you do. You are either going to run and hide, or you're going to be badgered until long after hell freezes over."

"And," Dale added, "neither you nor any of your deputies want to ever show your face in Clayborne County. We find you there, and there's a jail cell that you will be calling home."

Paul took his turn. "If I ever catch you somewhere alone, likely as not, you'll learn a lot about what dead feels like."

Before they left, just to show the people there they were serious, they locked all four of the men in the cell they were holding Lisa in, and took the keys for the cells with them. Lisa got the honor of tossing the keys into a large pond on the way back to Kingsburg.

As soon as they were there, Mack made the calls to the right lawyers, and the multiple lawsuits against sheriff Tod Mcintire, his department, and his county, were started.

Mack was sure he wouldn't win them all, but knew the ones he did win would hurt them a lot, as would their legal bill. This was one of the rare times Mack was glad to have too much money. He didn't have to worry about the money, either way.

CHAPTER 8

It was relatively peaceful for a couple of weeks. The worst thing that Mack and Lisa had to do was sit in a couple of depositions with all the lawyers, along with Sheriff Tod Mcintire and his three deputies. They made every attempt to claim that Lisa was way out of line when she was arrested.

That claim, however, was soon stifled by Mack's lawyers. First of all, they had a witness who saw them forcibly arrest Lisa without cause, especially since she was driving with her lights and siren on. Also, his lawyers surprised everyone on their side with videos of what went down at Sheriff Mcintire's office. Dale and all the deputies were wearing body cameras. Even Lisa.

"So," said the lead of Mack's lawyers, "either you all stop your lies, or we're going to file attempted rape charges against all four of you. And the truth is, my clients don't give even one damn whether you stop your lies and settle, or go to jail."

The opposition knew they were beaten. Their only question was should they settle or gamble on jail. After a short private meeting, they decided to try and settle. If the four men ended up with jail time, that would for sure cost them the civil case.

They made an offer to settle for half what they were being sued for. It didn't take any time for Mack to answer that. It was no, absolutely not. After a few more hours of deliberations, they finally settled on three quarters of the amount in the multiple lawsuits.

When it was all over one of the lawyers asked Mack what they were going to do with the money. "Easy," Mack answered, "give most of it to environmental organizations and the local food shelf."

"Really? It's a lot of money. I'd think you'd keep it all. Especially after what they tried to do to Lisa."

"We've gotten our satisfaction from beating them. Making them pay until it hurts is what matters. We don't need to spend their money to feel good about the revenge we got."

Dale had his own thoughts about it. "I'm not surprised about the way you're dealing with the money, just disappointed that you aren't going to rub it in their faces more."

"But I am," Mack said. "Opening day of the fishing season is coming up soon. Lisa and I are renting a house boat on the big lake, up in Sheriff Tod Mcintire's part of the world. We're going fishing for the weekend. Nothing but steaks and champagne for the entire time. All on the money we won from them."

"I don't think that's a very good idea, Mack. You know they'll be gunning for you. It'll be easier for them to get away with their dirty work out on that lake than it would be on land somewhere."

"Probably it would, if we were going to be out there alone. But we won't be. We're going to have three boats out on the lake. The other two will have two deputies and you and Paul. I will be hiring all of you at overtime rates, so Clayborne County won't be a problem. And don't you worry about me spending the money. I'm holding enough of it from the lawsuit to pay for the whole weekend.

When he made the arrangements for himself and Lisa for their fishing weekend, Mack pretended to try to keep what they were doing a secret. What he was actually doing was intentionally making mistakes in is efforts to ensure that Sheriff Tod Mcintire knew what he was doing.

Dale handled the arrangements for the other two boats, and he didn't make any mistakes when he did. No one other than the six people involved knew what they were really doing.

They were careful though, to have six other deputies involved. They were given throw away cell phones and instructed to keep them on and open for the entire weekend. They would be given instructions on what to do at the time they were needed, if they were needed.

So it was with great expectations that the three boats left their docks, about an hour apart, that Friday evening. They converged out near the middle of the large, but shallow, lake, about two hundred yards apart.

The first night was quiet, as was the first day. Supper that night, on all three boats, was fresh caught fish. It was breaded and deep fried, and served with french fries and salad.

It was a delicious and satisfying meal. When everyone on the boats went to bed that night, it was with nerves on edge anyway. If anything was going to happen, it would be tonight.

Mack knew it would be extremely stupid for both he and Lisa to go to sleep at the same time. He took the first watch. He didn't have to wait long. He expected the men who attacked them to sneak up to this boat as quietly as possible. Instead, because they thought Mack and Lisa were out there alone, they felt confident in attacking from their boats running full speed without any concern about the noise.

It was a huge mistake of their part. The noise not only warned Mack and Lisa, it warned the men in the other two boats. As the sheriff's two boats grew close to Mack and Lisa, so did Mack's two defenders.

Caught by surprise, the two attack boats only fired a couple of shots at Mack and Lisa before they started to flee for their lives. It was a losing proposition. Along with everything else that went into Mack's planning, was ensuring the he rented the fastest boats offered for rent anywhere on the lake.

They cornered both attack boats in a small bay on the far side of the lake. Some of the men in those boats decided that they were better off trying to shoot their way out than getting arrested would be.

It was another mistake. Dale always made sure that everyone, male or female, who was part of his department, trained enough to be proficient with their weapons.

Sheriff Tod Mcintire's men didn't make the effort. They spent most of their time sitting around doing little or nothing. The only time they were seriously active is when they were raping some innocent young girl who was unable to defend herself.

Once they realized, after three of them were lying dead, that they were severally out gunned, they surrendered as a single bunch. Most of the Jackstone's sheriff's deputies were among those either arrested or dead. Sheriff Tod Mcintire wasn't among them.

As much as his men were willing to talk, they didn't get him. He simply disappeared. They did, however, get the location of the old farmhouse they were currently using to hold captured girls.

They found six girls there, being prepared for shipment to Georgia.   Hoping they'd brought an end to the local human trafficking, they all went back to their normal duties. It was a far more relaxed environment than it had been for a long time, with everyone enjoying it. Everyone but Mack. Something in his gut was eating at him. He didn't mention his feelings to anyone. Not even Lisa. He was waiting until there was something more concrete than his own feelings to go on.

CHAPTER 9

They were an unhappy bunch. Losing the men who supplied them was bad. The loss of the girls was even worse. What would have been a small fortune for most people had been invested in them, and the sale price to their most valued customer was in the millions.

Providing the right kind of entertainment for employees where it was desperately needed wasn't cheap, anymore than it was always easy to find. The loss by both sides was putting a lot of pressure on the people who normally provided the merchandise offered in the exchange.

The head of this human trafficking bunch, a man named Barry Olson, wanted to know how and why it happened.

"What can you tell me about how all these problems got started?" he asked the man on the other end of the line, which was in a town called Baptism Towers. He was the current leader of the human trafficking group in Minnesota and its surrounding states.

"It was all Sheriff Tod Mcintire's doing. Seems he had some sort of vendetta against the Clayborne County's sheriff's department. He especially hated a couple of the deputies. Mack Thomas was one, and he hated his wife, Lisa, even more."

"I thought you said it was a couple of deputies he hated," Barry complained. "Then you bring a guys wife into it."

"Sorry. I said it wrong. His wife, Lisa, is the other deputy. It seems as though, when they get involved in anything going on, it's always bad news for whoever it is they're going after."

"If that's the way it is, why the hell don't you people get rid of them?"

"We've tried," Jerry told him. "Believe me, we've tried. In fact, several different groups have tried. A lot of those people were professionals with good records of job performance. Most of them ended up dead."

"I think you'd best try again. We've got to put a stop to this kind of interference. Our business is far too important to let some small time cops give us so much grief."

"We can try, but we don't really have anyone with the kind of talent that's going to be able to take them out."

"Well, I do. I'll be sending them to you. They'll get the job done."

"Okay, but just so you know, once you start with them, you'll have a war on your hands."

"Not a problem. Before my people are done, there won't be a Clayborne County Sheriff's Department."

As soon as Barry ended his conversation, he turned to the no longer sheriff, Tod Mcintire. "You heard my end of the conversation, so you know pretty much what we were talking about. What can you tell me about this hotshot Mack Thomas and his wife, Lisa? Are they really as bad as Jerry said, or is he full of bullshit?"

"They can be a problem. Much as I hate them, I have to give them credit. They're smart, tough, good with guns, and have a way of staying a step ahead of people trying to take them out. If that's your plan, use your best men. And tell them before they go, to use their best talents when they get there. They don't, and it will cost them."

"I'll do that. You can tell them all about Mack and Lisa, along with the rest of that sheriff's department on the way there."

"Why am I going? I'm not an expert assassin."

"You're going as a guide. You know the landscape and the people. That knowledge will give my guys more of an edge than they will have without that knowledge."

"Well, okay, if you really think it'll help."

"I wouldn't be sending you if I didn't."

Tod tried hard to believe the reasons Bert told him he was going, but he knew they were only partly true. He'd screwed up when he went after Lisa so hard, and this was a test to see if they'd keep him around. This time he knew, there'd be no second chances. He simply couldn't make any more mistakes.

As he thought about his trip back to Minnesota, it concerned him. He was wanted there now, so if he was recognized it would be disastrous. One of the few things he'd done right was to stop shaving his face, and start shaving his head. It changed his appearance a great deal. Even so, he knew he'd have to be very careful about showing his face anywhere. But especially in Clayborne County. There wasn't anyone there in law enforcement, who didn't hate him.

He was correct in his evaluation of the feelings of law enforcement toward him. He was universally hated. People who dealt in human trafficking, at least in a place like Minnesota, were considered to be about the lowest form of life in existence. And no one's opinion on that subject was stronger than Lisa Thomas's. Her feelings toward those people were pure hatred. If they also committed rape and she caught them in the act, their lives tended to be short ones.

She was thinking about the people who committed such terrible crimes as she stopped the second RV that day. It had become a habit of her's to pull them over for even the slightest reason. It started when she chased one over three counties, and ended up in a jail cell for doing it. That RV was being used by the local human trafficking ring.

This particular stop on this day proved to be a quick one. It was obviously a young family on their way for a long weekend camping trip. So she gave them a verbal warning about their cracked taillight lens, and sent them on their way.

After they were gone, she opened the door on her pickup to get in. For no particular reason, she momentarily stopped and watched the next few cars as they drove by her. As a new, custom van went by, the man in the passenger seat caught her eye.

For some reason, his full beard and bald head didn't seem to blend together. The balance just wasn't there. Seeing him made her shiver. It was almost as if he was somehow evil. The look on his face when he spotted her seemed to add to the feelings he gave her. The fact that all of the several men in the van suddenly looked at her seemed every bit as strange.

She sighed at her thoughts, and wondered if her job as deputy sheriff might be affecting her brain. She wasn't sure, but she wondered if her life filled with constant danger was making her a bit paranoid.

If so, was it worth it. She didn't need to work at a job. Especially not this one. She could easily quit. Mack certainly wouldn't object. And if she did, she'd have no trouble working full-time on their ranch. Having been raised on a dairy farm, she'd worked with cattle since she was a kid. It was also something she loved and was good at.

She loved gardening too, so she could spend part of her time working in the large family garden. There was plenty of additional work to be done in the fields where Mack's father Ben raised organic vegetables for market.

That lifestyle seemed awful tempting at times like this, when certain people sent those creepy/crawly feelings up her spine. After giving it some thought though, she knew she couldn't quit. There were too many times she'd been able to do some real good.

So she resigned herself to hanging on to what she had. A job important enough to provide genuine satisfaction at the end of most days. "So," she thought, "forget the creepy man in the van with the beard and no hair." That thought alone made her feel better, and she breathed easier for the rest of the day.

The easy breathing ceased at the end of the day when she told Mack about the van, the men in it, and the feelings it gave her.

"I don't think it was something weird that gave you those feelings, Lisa," Mack told her. "I can't prove it, nor will I claim that I'm for sure right, but it's been my feeling all along that the human trafficking people are still operating in Minnesota."

"You mean you think that van full of men I saw today is part of them?"

"Like I said, it's not something I'm positive of, but my gut says it's likely. Did any of those men seem to recognize you?"

"I don't know if his look was one of recognition or not," she said, as her own gut feeling was sending her a warning, "but in that short instant our eyes met, I did get the feeling that the bald guy with the face full of hair hated me."

"The more we talk, the more I'm sure they are part of it. Be my guess, they're here in some capacity for the traffickers. And although I don't know what that is, I'm sure that it has something to do with you."

"Why me?"

"Because you had the most to do with bringing the sheriff and his men down. Not only did we do that, mostly because of you, but we also rescued all those girls. That cost them plenty."

"What you're saying isn't it, Mack, that you think I'm going to be a target again?"

"Yes, in that you're probably their primary target. I have no doubts though, that I'm not far behind you, and that the whole department isn't far behind me. If it was just you they were after, there wouldn't be near so many of them."

"What do you think we should do about it?"

"I'm not exactly sure yet. I want to sleep on it before I decide what we can do about it. I'd like to talk it over with Dale too. So when I have coffee with him in the morning, I want you there. I think it's important he hears what you have to say."

"But will Dale approve of me being there?"

"That's not something he can approve or disapprove of. So make sure that you're there. It matters."

CHAPTER 10

Dale was surprised when Lisa sat down across from him while he was having his morning coffee break at Katy's Kafe on main street in Kingsburg. It was, and had been for a number of years, a ritual for him and Mack to have coffee together. It wasn't something they did every morning, but did every morning possible.

"What brings you here, Lisa?" he asked.

"Mack, mostly. I didn't think I should be here, but he insisted."

"Is there a reason for this? Not that I mind. I always enjoy your company."

"Yes, Dale, there is a reason. I'd rather not talk about it before he gets here though. He's better at explaining things than I am."

"I'm not so sure about that. You've always been as articulate as any of us." Before he could say anything else, Mack joined them.

"Sorry I'm a little late," he said. "I had to check out a custom van driving through town."

"Is there a special reason for checking on a custom van now?" Dale asked.

"There is," Mack answered. "Custom vans have a lot to do with the reason I asked Lisa to join us today."

"Really? Did you have a problem with one you stopped or something?" Dale asked her.

"No," Mack answered for her. "It was something she saw in one." He turned to her. "Tell him everything you told me last night, Lisa. And include your feelings about it."

Before she started her explanation, the waitress came to take their breakfast order. Since Mack and Lisa already ate with their family, they only ordered coffee.

Lisa then gave Dale a detailed explanation of what she saw in the van the previous day, including the look on the bald man's face and the way the other men in the van suddenly turned to stare at her.

"And based on that observation of a single van, you now believe we have a serious problem? One which you think will affect the entire department? I've learned to respect your gut feelings, Lisa. You've been right too many times not too. But this one is a definite stretch."

This was the right time, Mack was sure, to open up on him. So he did. "The thing is," he began, "I not only agree with her, I feel even more strongly than she does that we have a serious problem. I'm not talking about one that will just eat up resources and cost the county in overtime. What we're facing here, *right now,* is a crisis that will cost lives if we don't react the right way."

"I hope you're exaggerating in order to get my attention, Mack. I definitely don't want to believe you're serious about what you just said."

Mack sighed heavily, shook his head, and leaned back in his chair. The look he gave Dale then would have been most upsetting to anyone else. It certainly didn't give him anything close to a positive feeling about their discussion. The waitress returned with their coffee and Dale's breakfast before he answered.

"The thing is," Mack said, "I think that van was full of goons, trained killers, probably sent here by the mob out east. What we did when we broke up Tod Mcintire's bunch, most likely hurt them a lot. We rescued several girls they were expecting to buy, and either dried up or at minimum, slowed down future deliveries."

"So you think they're here to kill some of us?"

"No, I don't. I think they're probably here to kill as many of us as possible. If not all of us. I have no doubts, either, that Lisa and I are on the top of their list. You are likely close behind us on that list."

"That's a hell of a lot to believe from one short look at that van."

"Not really, Dale. For me, it's exactly what I've been expecting all along."

"Really? Why?"

"We did one hell of a job when we took out Sheriff' Mcintire's men. But we didn't get him. That was a worry. At the same time, I knew that the mob behind all this was going to look for a way to stop anymore interference from us. But to do that, they had to learn who we were. Who was best to tell them that?"

"Sometimes I hate it, Mack, when your ideas sound so reasonable. It would be Sheriff Tod Mcintire. He'd be the best to tell them all about us." Dale paused a moment, scratched his head, looked at Mack first, then Lisa. "What do you think?" he asked her.

"Mack's right about all of it."

"What do you think our next step should be?"

"Well, normally a person in my position would tell you about all the ways we should get ourselves better prepared to defend ourselves. And I guess we should do that. But I think what we need to do even more is go on the offense. Let's not wait for them to move in on us. We need to go on the hunt for them."

"That's pretty strong, Lisa. We'll need to get more evidence to be able to do that."

"We've already got some," Mack said. "To start with, I'd bet long odds that the bald guy Lisa saw was Tod Mcintire. He's a wanted man now. The chances of any of the mob boys not having some kind of record is highly unlikely. That makes it illegal for them to carry firearms. Even if it doesn't, the guns they'll be carrying will likely as not be illegal anyway. And finally, if we push them hard enough, they'll break the law trying to get to us."

"How do you plan to push them? We don't even know where they are."

"Not exactly, and maybe not even for sure. But I'm betting they're not that far away. I think we can rattle their cage some, just by visiting Jackstone county."

"You are looking to make some trouble there, aren't you, Mack?"

"I am. Let's raise some real hell up there. And see what it shakes out of their corrupt activities."

Lisa voiced her opinion of Mack's plan. "I think," she said, speaking directly too Dale, "that Mack's ideas on what to do about the problem are pretty much the only thing we can do that will work. Like I said, we need to be aggressive if we're going to get those guys before they get us."

"Well, suppose we go ahead with this. Who do you plan to have working with you, Mack?"

"Me, I hope," Lisa interrupted. "Since I'm a target anyway, there's no reason you can't let me work with you, Mack."

"Actually, there is, Lisa. You and I are too close to do this kind of work together. Especially when it's so dangerous. If I have you with me doing this, I'll be so worried about you I'll likely make a mistake. It could get us killed."

"I think I've earned the right to be directly involved," she complained. "And I don't believe you have the right to tell me I can't."

Mack shrugged his shoulders, then said, "I'm not telling you can't. I know better than anyone that you've earned the right to be involved. I just don't think it would be wise for you to ride with me. As I said, it would take me off my game too far."

"If I'm not riding with you, who will?"

"I'm going to ask Paul. No matter how you look at it, he's the most experienced person in our department. It will be a huge asset during an operation like this."

"Well, who will be riding with me?" She asked.

"Me," Dale answered. "You will be riding with me."

His answer took her and Mack by surprise, but after a moment Mack smiled. "As a deputy in the department, I'd say that you just got the best man for the job, Lisa. As your husband, I have to say that Dale just made me a much relieved man. With him riding with you, I won't be worrying that things could go wrong for you out there because someone did something stupid."

"How are you going to be able to get away for long enough at a time?" Lisa asked.

Dale gave her a broad smile. "That's easy. When you were the fill-in sheriff while I was gone, the changes you made in the office routine has allowed me a lot more time out of the office than I ever had before."

"She is good at organizing just about anything," Mack said, "isn't she?"

"Definitely. So good, that if she wasn't even better as a deputy out and about every day, I'd make her office manager and give her a substantial raise."

"Please, Dale, don't ever do that to me. I don't ever want to manage anything that has me giving work direction to people day after day. I love what I do now."

"I know that, Lisa. And you're more than just good at it. So I'll never so much as offer you the job."

"Good. Now what are we going to do to be sure we've increased security for everyone in the department?"

"I think we'll have a meeting tomorrow morning, first thing, to go over it with as many of us as we can. They all deserve to have a say in what ever decisions we make. But now, it's time for me to get back to the office, just like it's time for you to get back out there and earn your pay."

Dale's last comment was enough to make then all smile as they left Katy's. Money was the last reason Lisa and Mack were sheriff's deputies.

CHAPTER 11

Mack wasn't completely satisfied with the meeting. Talk was nearly all about increasing security and very little about going after those involved in the human trafficking. He appreciated the need for ensuring the safety of everyone who was part of the sheriff's department, and agreed with every measure they could take to manage that. But he also felt that they needed to aggressively go after all those involved in the trafficking, if they were ever going to return to their normal routines.

When he left the meeting, he knew it was up to him to come up with the ideas and plans needed to bring an end to the constant threat they were now facing.

At the same time, with the weather back to what would be called normal in Minnesota, with the snow melted, and the flood waters receded, Mack and Lisa decided to spend a Saturday morning at the wildlife refuge. At a quick glance, it still looked like a burned out, desolate landscape. Looking close though, the recovery going on after the previous years devastating fire seemed remarkable.

Native grasses dominated. Small, broadleaf plants followed, and many of them were already blooming, filling many small areas with color. The few trees that survived the fire were beginning to leaf out. And everywhere birdsong and insect hum could be heard. Not with the volume found before the fire, but there nonetheless.

They parked in a lot at the head of a trail and followed it. Even after living with the refuge for a year after the fire, it still felt strange to them to be walking the whole time on open ground. Before the fire, the trail they were on was wooded from the parking lot on.

Even so, they quickly were seeing increasing signs of animal life. Bees were active on all the blooming plants, as were butterflies. Small critters like chipmunks and ground squirrels appeared in larger numbers than they expected. Twice they saw snakes. One was a common garter snake, who rapidly scurried away. The other snake was a bull snake, who took his own good time moving away from them. He left the impression that he was sure the worst they could do to him was annoy him.

As the trail took them further into the refuge, they spotted a pair of coyotes up on a small hill. They were standing there quietly, watching Mack and Lisa. They didn't bother to leave the hill until Mack and Lisa were within fifty feet of them. Mack was somewhat disappointed in them when they showed such a lack of fear. He knew their own confidence around humans was dangerous for them. There were simply too many people with guns who would love nothing more than to kill a pair of coyotes.

Mack was thankful that the small herd of deer reacted the opposite. As soon as they spotted Mack and Lisa, they were gone, moving fast, but with a grace and beauty that could almost take one's breath away.

Stopping to watch them, Lisa took Mack's hand. "It's too bad, isn't it," she said, "that such a small number of us humans are able to appreciate a sight like that.

"It is," he agreed. "But it's something that's never going to change. Not to any degree."

"Why do you think that is, Mack? Why can't most people learn to appreciate other life forms?"

"Because of the way they're taught. We're told from a very young age that humans are the only life form that matters. Everything else, no matter what it is, is only here for us to use. For too many people the use thing includes all manner of abuse. It doesn't matter to them what they have to do in order to use it. If they think they need it, or simply just want it, the amount of destruction they cause to get it doesn't matter. All that matters is they get what they want."

"What makes people think and act that way?" she asked. "I've never been able to understand where that attitude comes from, or why so many people have it."

"All too much of it comes directly from religion. We're supposed to be created in God's image. So no matter what we do to the environment and to all other life forms doesn't matter. Only human life matters. And for too many of the rich, only the lives of rich humans matter. I could go on about this for hours, but it wouldn't change anything. So I'll let it go at that."

In the past, Lisa disagreed with Mack when he said negative things about religion. This time she remained quiet. Too many of the things she thought she was absolutely right about, no longer seemed so right. Living with Mack, she'd learned how to do something too seldom done by most people. She had learned how to question. No longer could faith alone give her the answers she all too often needed, or simply wanted.

The gradual change in her ideas and opinions was something Mack had been seeing since they'd fallen in love. And even though he appreciated it, he was wise enough to refrain from commenting on it. He didn't want to do anything to upset the change that was happening. As far as his loving her, that wouldn't change even if she wasn't growing the way she was. But he had to admit to himself that watching her grow in understanding of so many things, including the things he so strongly believed in, was something special.

"Mack, I wonder sometimes how you manage to keep yourself in balance. On one hand, you're rich. Yet, you rarely have much if anything good to say about the rich. It's kind of a contradiction, isn't it?"

"A big one. Initially, when I came into the money I didn't earn or deserve, I just tried to give it all away. It seemed to be too big a burden to carry. Then things kept happening that allowed me to do some good with it. Enough so, that I decided it wasn't so bad to hang onto some of it. Then I figured out how to keep a certain balance in that wealth and still help people."

"I know. And I know that if you could get rid of it and still help when help was needed, you would."

Mack paused a moment then, thinking about the large amount of money he had, and couldn't help compare it with the beauty of the new life starting up all around him. He once more realized how much more valuable that life was than those dollars he had in the bank. Those thoughts defined his next comment.

"I would love to get rid of it, Lisa. I just wish I could figure out a way to use that money to bring an end to what's going on around here right now."

"I do too. You know how I feel about people, mostly it is men who are involved in human trafficking. As far as I'm concerned, the customers of those people are as bad. So are any of the incredible number of men who commit rape."

"And I don't blame you for that at all. If I were you, I'd hate them as much, or more, then you do. As it is, I have my own kind of hatred for them. What you went through should never have happened. It should never happen to anyone. And we should be doing a lot more about it than we've been doing."

"You're right. It shouldn't. It destroyed Terry," Lisa said, referring to a girl who was kidnapped and kept in the same place as she was. While there, they became friends. "You know, Mack, I've often wished I could meet the drug dealers who killed those men who kidnapped me. I'd like to thank them."

"You don't have to. The people who did it know that you're thankful for what they did."

"How could they possibly know that?"

"They do. Actually, I should say that they did. They're both gone now?"

"What do you mean, gone? Where'd they go?"

"I meant, they're dead now."

"How do you know that? Did you know them or something?"

"I did."

"Well, Mack, then tell me."

"I'm not so sure I should. It might bother you to know who it was."

"Well, now you have to tell me. I'll go nuts if you don't."

"I guess if I were in your position, I'd feel the same way. Your friend Terry killed one of them." He paused, not sure he should tell her about the other one.

Lisa only waited a couple of minutes before asking again, "So, who killed the other two?"

"Are you absolutely sure you want to know. It's going to shock you."

"I couldn't be more sure."

"It was your Grandfather. The detective who was handling the investigation made it look like it was drug dealers."

Lisa's eyes went wide and her mouth dropped open. Then, as the realization of it hit her, a gradual smile crept over her face. "Really, my grandpa did that. God, I wish I would have known it while he was still alive. I'd like to have been able to thank him, but even more than that, to tell him how proud I am of him. Eliminating those men from the face of the earth was probably the best thing he ever did in his whole life. And he lived a good life and did a lot of good things."

"I can't argue with that," Mack said, sighing heavily. "He was a good man. I could never fault him for what he did. Now, I especially can't, given what we're probably going to have to do in the near future."

"That sounded real serious," she said as she stepped slightly away from him, then turned her head up to look him in the eye. "What is it that you're thinking about doing?"

"Everything. I'm thinking about all of the people, the groups or gangs or mobs or whatever you want to call them. We can't just clean up the mess we've got here, we have got to go after everything. We need to start here, but we can't stop until we've taken it all the way."

"Come on, Mack, you're not serious, are you? What could we possibly do to the mob controlling the trafficking? There must be damn near as many of them as there are people in Kingsburg."

"I know, but that doesn't mean we can't do some damage. Their leaders are the worst of them. Having them gone could possibly be of benefit for the whole world. Not to mention getting them off our backs."

"I'm sure it would help us and the world, but how could we ever manage something like that? The distance between them and us alone, is enough to make it impossible."

"It's closer than it seems," Mack told her. "Much closer."

Watching the determined look on his face, Lisa got the feeling that he would without a doubt, come up with something that was ultimately more than anyone expected. The big questions were, what would it be, and how far would it go?

CHAPTER 12

Mack knew they needed one more meeting, but this one was going to be small. Only the people who were going to be directly involved in the next move made by the Clayborne County Sheriff's Department were asked to be there.

So it wasn't any big surprise to any of the four when they joined Dale at his morning coffee break at Katy's Kafe. Detective Paul Danielson was the first of them to speak.

"Given who's here this morning, I assume Mack's brought us together to discuss our next move."

"I would too," Lisa agreed. "I was sure that it was about that when he strongly suggest I stop here for coffee this morning."

"I figured it out as soon as you came inside, Lisa," Dale said. "You didn't even have to sit down at my table for me to know."

Mack couldn't help but smile at their comments. "Now that you've all figured out why we're here, let's talk about it."

"The first thing we need to decide," Dale suggested, "is when."

"I think in three days," Mack explained. "That will give Paul and I time to get ready."

"What kind of getting ready are you thinking about?"

"To start with, going three days without shaving. We definitely don't want to look like clean-cut, honest gentlemen. We need to give the impression that we're looking for trouble, preferably in the form of women who are for sale. At least, for a few hours, if not a full night."

"What about Dale and me?" Lisa asked. "What are we supposed to be?"

"A cute couple out for a little fun. People who come across as opposite of what Paul and I are as possible."

"Are you sure, Mack, that it's not going to bother you some, watching me flirt with Dale, and maybe some strangers. Because that's what I'll have to do to pull off the image you want us to have."

"Not this time. I fully trust you, Lisa, so even if I won't like watching it, I'll be able to deal with it."

"Don't worry too much, Mack," Dale told him. "We'll keep the flirting to a minimum. If for no other reason than Kathy would kill me if she ever thought there was even the slightest reality to it."

Paul decided to add some levity to the conversation. "You know, if there's going to be flirting done with Lisa, I wouldn't at all mind being the one to play her partner. I can't think of anything that would make this old man to feel young again, like flirting with Lisa would." He followed his comment with a laugh, to make sure Mack knew he was kidding.

Laugh or not, Lisa blushed anyway. Mack wasn't about to get upset about Paul's comment. He knew full well that most men would enjoy flirting with Lisa. Something about her went beyond her physical beauty. It was a something that still affected him everyday.

"If you guys keep talking this way," she said, "we might have to change this arrangement. Mack will have to accept me as his partner this time. I don't ever want to do something to hurt our relationship."

"It's going to be okay, Lisa." Mack simply looked at her for a moment, so she could see how much he loved and trusted her. Then he said, "What we're going to be doing is going to take all of us totally trusting each other. I've never had any reason to not trust any of you. So I think we can get passed the issue of flirting now, and get on with the plan."

They went over the plan then, and in a short time agreed on what they hoped to accomplish. They then left Katy's and each went their separate ways.

Lisa spent much of her day patrolling the four lane, looking for suspicious RVs and vans. It was a slow day though, and she only stopped one RV. All the rest of the traffic seemed normal. There was only one exception to her slow day.

Mack spent the day traveling around the county. The most exciting thing to happen to him was stopping a rather tipsy, middle age lady for careless driving. He rarely made traffic stops, but the car she was driving was weaving all over the road, giving him no choice but to stop her.

When he walked up to the driver's side of the car, she was unbuttoning the third button of her blouse, giving Mack a nice view. It was immediately obvious what she had in mind. It was a game he didn't want to play. She was more than attractive enough, but his loyalty to Lisa far out weighed any desire he might have for what she was about to offer. He also didn't want to ever have to deal with any accusations she might make later, after she sobered up.

So rather than even making any attempt to deal with her, he used his radio to request backup. As luck would have it, he was on a county road less than a mile from the highway. Lisa was the deputy who came to back him up.

"What's up?" she asked Mack when she joined him.

"The lady in the car was driving extremely erratically, so I pulled her over. When I approached her, she apparently had things in mind to convince me not to ticket her. I thought it best to have another deputy on hand when she's taken in. She's too drunk to drive, and I don't need to have anyone accusing me of something I'm not about to do. I've got a hell of a lot more important things to do than deal with a women trying to do what she's trying to do."

"Okay, Mack," Lisa said, unable to hide her grin. "I'll take care of it. I'd appreciate it though, if you'd stick around until I get her loaded into my pickup."

Mack did, and ended up assisting Lisa in loading the lady into her truck.

When they finished, Lisa couldn't help but tease him a little. "You know, Mack," she said, "from the condition she's in, you could have taken advantage without any problem. She's pretty enough, and she's already half undressed herself for you."

Mack blushed, shook his head, and said, "not in a million years. And you know it."

"I do, but after all that talk of flirting this morning, I thought it might be enough to really put you in the mood."

"It was, but the mood can only be taken care of tonight. By you."

"I know, and that fact makes me a happy woman." She gave him a quick kiss and left to take the errant woman to the station to either be picked up by someone, or sober up.

Mack waited for the wrecker to arrive to pick up the woman's car. While he waited his mind wandered around for a while, until it settled on thoughts of Lisa. They quickly made him smile.

CHAPTER 13

In the three days they waited, Paul's dark whiskers already covered his face, nearly hiding it. Mack's were a contrast. There were more than enough of them, but so light in color that he barely looked like he needed a shave, so they didn't do much to make him look rough. However, when added to the scars on his face' that he'd acquired his third day as a sheriff's deputy, from a shotgun wound, made up the difference in their appearance.

The clothes they wore were clean, but well worn. They went well with the hats they wore. Mack's was a twins hat and Paul's a vikings. Neither one of them were sports fans, but they filled out the overall effect they wanted.

Because his truck was equipped with lights, siren, and everything else a deputy sheriff could ever want, it was too obvious to use this time. Instead, Mack drove an extra pickup that was normally used around the farm/ranch for various jobs and errands. He didn't much like driving it, but it was decent cover for what they were trying to accomplish.

Dale drove a late model car he borrowed from the impound lot. He dressed in comfortable pair of slacks and short sleeved shirt. Lisa wore her black skirt with a special pocket in the back of the waist band. Inside the pocket was a switchblade knife, which retracted, rather than flipped out. It was a weapon which had proved useful in the past. To go with the skirt, she wore a filmy bra. It didn't show anything, but it made a man wish it did. Her white blouse was just semi-transparent enough to make her look as though it might be possible to get lucky with her. She was good enough an actress to fake a smile that completed the look. The only thing out of place about her clothes was her stockings. They were heavy enough to hide the derringer she carried inside them. No one noticed them though.

As always, it bothered Mack that Lisa was the main decoy again. The fact that she looked as beautiful as she did wasn't the problem. He was proud of her for that. The problem was the fear she might get hurt. At the same time, he knew she could take care of herself as well as anyone. More than that, he knew it was a waste of time trying to convince her to stay out of the way of dangerous situations. She'd made it clear to everyone involved that as long as she was part of law enforcement, she was going to enforce the law. And do whatever was necessary to do it.

To get to the place they planned to start their investigation, they drove north to Jackstone County, where Tod Mcintire was sheriff before he disappeared. Dale and Lisa were about ten minutes behind Mack and Paul. Their destination was the town called Baptism Towers. It was small, with a population of less than a thousand, but somehow managed to have its own police force. It consisted of the chief of police and one deputy. They were only active for ten hours a day, from noon to ten PM. They weren't anything that concerned Mack or the rest of them. All four of them knew the police there were decidedly ineffective.

The bar they planned to visit was called the Old Time Inn. It was old time only in the fact that it was beat-up just enough to appear old. Inside, the bar ran along the back wall. A series of six booths ran along the wall to the right. A pool table was near the left side, and tables for four filled the rest of the place. Mack and Paul sat at the bar when they went in.

They ordered beer, which was served in heavy, iced mugs, with handles big enough to make them easy to handle. Four guys were playing pool, so they turned to watch the game. Two other young men, sitting at a nearby table, watched the game too, but with intermittent glances at Mack and Paul. The two men were doing their best to come across as tough guys, but failed to impress them.

They purposely ignored the watchers. What the two were doing wasn't unusual in this environment. They were in a small town's local bar and obvious strangers. Which made them invaders. So it wouldn't be unusual for any or all of the six men inside to try to start some trouble, if only to prove how macho they were. No matter that six on two wasn't particularly macho.

That, again, wasn't something that concerned either Mack or Paul in the slightest. Paul was neither young nor fast, but he was still strong and had many years and opportunities to learn how to deal with this kind of situation. The odds of even three of the men there being able to take him were slim. Mack, on the other hand, didn't have as much experience. He did, however, have a lot of training in self defense, was big, and stronger than most who were his size or bigger. And as much as he preferred to avoid fights, he knew how to end them in his favor.

But it remained a quiet place until Dale and Lisa arrived. She came in first, holding his hand. She gave the impression that she was very much enjoying his company as she led him to a table in the middle of the room. She sat in the chair next to him, rather than the one across from him, and rested her hand on his shoulder. She was doing her best to make it look like they had something special going between them.

The bartender, who watched them constantly from the time they came in the door, actually went to their table to take their drink order. As soon as he reached their table it was obvious why he did it. His eyes roamed over her face and upper body constantly, and his face quickly filled with lust. She did a good job of ignoring his constant stare. She only acknowledged him when she ordered her drink.

Lisa and Dale looked at the menus while the bartender filled their drink orders. When he returned with Lisa's glass of white wine and Dale's glass of beer, they each ordered a bacon cheeseburger and fries. As soon as the bartender reluctantly left to put their burgers on the grill, the two men sitting at a table decided to join them. They made no attempt to hide what they had in mind. Lisa didn't hide how she felt about their company. She sneered at them, purposely letting them know she was annoyed with them.

Mack nudged Paul, letting him know that this was the start of the trouble they knew was coming. This town and this bar was already suspect for a lot of nasty things happening, and they were there to learn as much about what was going on as possible. Especially they were looking for a connection to the human trafficking going on in that part of Minnesota. There was no doubt in Mack's mind, that these were the kind of men who would be involved with it. If not directly, then in some sort of peripheral role. They hoped that Dale, and especially Lisa, could get the men talking.

Instead, the two men sat down, and the man sitting next to Lisa didn't waste any time to show his intentions. Talking wasn't one of them. He gave her a leering grin and said, "Well, Babe, I think fate brought you here to me. Either that, or I just got lucky today, 'cause me and you are definitely going to have some fun." He pushed an arm around her neck and reached for her breast with the other.

She wasn't expecting anyone to move that quickly or aggressively. She knew what they were there to do, but she wasn't going to allow him to touch her, even if the original plan was for her to be a bit of a flirt. She didn't mind attracting their attention that way, to get them to start talking, but she wasn't going to be touched by a creep like him. It was retaliation time.

She quickly stood up, removing his arm as she did. She grabbed his middle finger of that hand, and with a controlling twist, broke it. He screamed in pain. Tears filled his eyes as he doubled over, holding his finger tightly, trying to stop the pain.

"You, bitch," he threatened, "you're going to pay for that."

"You put your hands on me again," she told him, her tone of voice making it obvious to everyone there that she meant it, "And you'll have a lot worse hurt than a broken finger."

He suddenly growled, straightened up, and lunged at her. No longer having any interest in putting up with any of his macho, bully-boy games, she easily sidestepped him and as he flew by her, slammed her foot into the side of his knee. He went down, out of commission for the foreseeable future. His knee wasn't broken, but was torn up enough to keep him down.

Everyone, including even Mack, was surprised by her quick and total response to the man's attempts to molest her. Even though it wasn't part of what they'd planned, he wasn't at all upset with her. He was, instead, extremely proud of her reactions. It also set the tone for the action that followed.

Dale stood up, along with the other man sitting at their table.

"You just made the wrong move, Lady," he said, struggling to sound tough. It was a struggle he lost. "For what you just did, you're going to pay." He pushed his face into an angry expression. "You ain't gonna pull that kind of shit on my friend," he threatened in a voice with a bit of a squeak.

"I think you'd better just back off," Dale told him, his anger showing. "All we came in here for was something to eat. Now leave us alone, before you get hurt."

The second man just tried to laugh, then when that didn't quite make it, motioned to the four men at the pool table. All of them had already stopped their game. They were just watching, until they were motioned to come to Dale and Lisa's table. With their faces filled with evil grins, they walked over to it. Two of them grabbed Dale from behind and held him. Two others grabbed Lisa. There was no doubt about what they planned to do to Dale, and when they were done, what they wanted to do to Lisa.

Cocky as they tried to be, it bothered all five of the trouble makers when neither Lisa nor Dale showed the slightest sign of fear. In fact, the look of total contempt they got from Lisa confused them. In the past, when they'd taken advantage of women, they showed their fear. For most of the abused women, it was a lot of fear.

Mack and Paul left their bar stools and joined the group. "That's more than enough," Paul told them. "Let go of both of them, while you still can. Without getting hurt, that is."

"Or what, Asshole. You gonna take on all of us?"

"No. We aren't going to take you twits on. We're going to beat the living shit out of you." Mack answered, giving them his best smile.

It took every bit of strength the four men had, to hold on to Lisa and Dale. Of the two men who started the trouble, only one was still standing. Mack turned to him, since he was the only one of the six men not occupied with something. His look was now confused. All of his previous belligerence was gone, and it was easy to see that he had no idea what to do next.

Mack moved in close to him and said, "Well?"

The man backed away from the table. Mack put his hand on the shoulder of one of the men holding Lisa. He used all his strength and pulled him away. This gave Lisa the opening she wanted. She was still angry. She had no tolerance for men who believed they had some kind of right to do anything to a woman they wanted to do. So she decided to let the second man who'd been holding on to her know how she felt. He was slow to do anything when she pulled loose of him, so she did the quickest and easiest thing she could do to him. She jabbed him, with her fingers, in the eyes. She knew from the way it felt that it would be a long time, if ever, before he would see again. He screamed in pain and fell to his knees. Tempted as she was to kick his teeth out, she left him on the floor with his pain.

Mack didn't use any special moves on the man he pulled away from Lisa. He just hit him in the gut, doubling him over, then held him by the hair as he brought a knee into his face. His nose made a loud crunch when it was smashed against the knee. Like the other two before him, he dropped to the floor, moaning loudly.

At the same time Mack and Lisa were busy, Paul moved in on one of the men holding Dale. Again, no fancy moves. He just slammed the palm of his hand into his face, and his nose made the same crunch as the other nose when it broke. Paul followed with the side of his fist to the man's temple and he was done.

Dale simply drove his fist under his man's chin, knocking him out instantly. That left the confused man standing. Paul looked at the bartender and held up his hand, his palm facing his direction. The bartender nodded, telling Paul he understood, and stayed behind the bar. He was wise enough to stay out of the fight. There was no doubt in his mind about the stupidity of going against these strangers who had invaded his bar. And given the tension he felt from the current situation, his lust for Lisa disappeared.

Mack and Dale sat the confused man down, to question him about the state of things in Jackstone County. The only emotion he had left was fear. It left him certain that the best he'd get from the four people staring at him was a bad beating. The thought of it so terrified him that he wet his pants. This was situation he'd never, in his wildest imaginings, expected to find himself. He and his friends had always controlled every other trouble they started. And never had he seen a woman they wanted to use fight back. Sure, some of them screamed, and all of them cried. But fight back, never. And even though he'd just seen her do it, he still couldn't believe she could beat two of them.

In every fight he and his friends had ever started, they'd always won. Anyone on the other side was always the victim. After all, it's hard to lose a fight when you out number your opponent two to one or better. And all the women involved always left the place a lot more humble than they were when they came in. Now, here he was, at the mercy of these four people. People who knew how to take care of themselves.

Because he was sheriff, and technically the leader, Dale started the questioning. "What you're going to have to do now," he told the sitting man, "is tell us about the women brought to this county by human traffickers. If you don't, it's going to be hard for me to describe the condition you'll be in when this conversation is over."

"I don't know nothin' about stuff like that."

Before Dale could say anything more to him, the bartender, who until now had stayed out of it, interrupted. "He really doesn't know anything. None of these guys do. They're just country boys with not enough real things to keep themselves busy and out of trouble."

"No," Mack argued, "they aren't just country boys. They're bully boys. Cowards really. This bar of yours could be something decent, but you let trash like these guys hang out here. That makes no sense to me."

"If I could get rid of them, I would. But this is only six of them. There's lots more. I've tried to sell the place, but the reputation it has kills any sale possible. So I deal with it best I can, until I can afford to walk away. The one decent thing they do, is pay their bar bills, so in spite of everything, I'm doing well enough to retire in a couple of years."

"It's just fine," Mack said, "that you claim this clown doesn't know anything. What about you? What do you Know?"

"Not a whole hell of a lot. There's been a lot of rumors, but nothing that I could ever say is real or not. The thing is though, I'm fairly sure there's a place out in the country that's a brothel. I don't know much about it. Only bits and pieces I pick up from conversations people at the bar have."

"That's not what we're looking for," Mack explained. "What we want to know about is the human trafficking that's going on. There's all too many young women being taken and forced into a life of prostitution."

"I understand that, but if you go out there, there might be someone who can tell you something."

"Why do you think that?"

"Because they're basically in the same business. Given that they're operating in the same area, it seems like they might be somehow connected. Or at least have some knowledge of each other. That's the tone of some of the conversations I've overheard anyway."

Mack couldn't help but sigh as he listened to the bartender. He didn't think that prostitution was in itself evil. Nor were the women who willingly practiced the trade. The problem he had with the business were the men involved who all too frequently controlled, and most often mistreated, the women. They were nearly one hundred percent the lowest of the lowlife monsters anywhere. He'd never met a pimp he didn't want to lock up for life.

So he decided that as much as he disliked the idea, they were going to visit the place. The bartender gave them directions to where he thought the brothel was, but couldn't guaranty they would get them there.

When he finished telling them everything he knew, the men on the floor began to stir. The two Lisa had dealt with were still disabled. The one with the broken finger and damaged knee still wasn't able to put together enough coordination to stand. The other one, who could now see, but with everything too blurry to identify, only managed to sit himself down in a chair. The two with broken noses asked for towels to wipe up the blood now covering their faces. The one Dale dealt with was still dealing with a brain in a fog bank.

The one left, sitting in his wet pants and still trembling, was no longer able to talk. His fear was so great that it took his voice. When they looked at him to further question him, the smell surrounding him changed their minds. His fear had grown to the point that his bowels broke loose. The odor from it was almost overwhelming.

Even though they hadn't accomplished as much as they hoped, Mack, Lisa, Paul, and Dale decide to call it a day. The bartender gave his word that he wouldn't tell anyone about their conversation, and the six men who were so sure they were going to have fun with Lisa, didn't really have anything to tell anyone. Even if they'd heard anything that registered, the last thing they'd ever want anybody to know was how bad they'd gotten their asses kicked. By only three men, and a woman capable of besting any one of them in any kind of fight.

Lisa was out the door first, with Mack right behind her. Since they weren't going to check out the brothel that day, Lisa decide to ride back with Mack. But before they reached the pickup he was driving, two men drove in.

They noticed Lisa right away, and being who and what the were, they were sure they were going to have some fun. One of them quickly pushed by Mack and tried to grab Lisa. She was as thoroughly tired of their game as a person could get tired of anything.

"If I were you," she told the man standing in front of her, as she reached into the rear pocket of the skirt she was wearing, "I would definitely turn around and get the hell away from me."

He laughed. "Well now, there ain't much you can do about it if I don't, now is there?"

"Actually, there is. If you put one hand on me, you for sure will regret it."

This time neither Mack nor Dale nor Paul went to her defense. They just watched. The man hadn't seen Dale or Paul, and didn't realize that Mack had already disabled his friend.

So he made his mistake and reached for Lisa's arm with the intention of pulling her to him. She didn't waste any motion. She simply slashed his wrist before he knew she had the switchblade in her hand. It cut deep and the blood poured out of him.

She pushed the knife blade quickly across each of his cheeks. Just deep enough to leave permanent scars. "You want more? The next stop for this blade will be your throat."

He looked at his wrist, pouring blood on the ground, and staggered back. "My god," he whined, "I'm going to bleed to death." He touched his face, then stared at the blood on his fingers, and his eyes went wide.

"Yes, you will die," Lisa told him, "unless you put a tourniquet on it."

He fainted then.

Paul put a tourniquet on his arm, while Mack called the local police. Since the police station was only a block away in the small town, and the chief rarely left it, he managed to get there in a few minutes after answering the call.

All four of them showed him their IDs immediately, so he didn't go through the charade of trying to arrest them. Lisa did the talking. She told him what happened, both inside the bar and out in the parking lot.

"So now that you've beaten up all these men," the chief complained, "you want me to clean up the mess."

"Yes, we sure do," she said. "It's a damn cinch we aren't going to."

"Well, you should, coming into my town the way you did, making all this trouble."

"The trouble was here before we ever got here. We just wanted to try to get some information about the human trafficking going on in this part of the state."

"There is no such thing going on around here," the chief protested. "This is a nice, quiet little town. We never have this kind of trouble. So I don't appreciate your accusations that we do."

It was more than obvious the chief was lying, so they gave up on him ever being cooperative. "Well then," Mack told him, "feel more than free to clean up this *quiet* little mess."

He, along with the other three, knew it was time to head for home. So they did. Lisa rode with Mack, and was quiet for the first few minutes. Then she asked, "Why aren't you anxious to check out the brothel? You know they'll be ready for us when we do check it out."

"They're ready and waiting for us now. In fact, I have no doubt they're waiting for us, with anything they don't want us to see, hidden away. If the bartender hasn't called them to warn them, one of the six creeps in the bar has."

"But the longer we wait, the more ready they're going to be."

"That'll work in their favor for the next two or three days. After that, they'll stop believing we're coming. That way, when we do pay them a visit, it won't be a complete surprise, but it'll be a lot more of one than if we went there today."

"Okay, Mack. That makes sense. But what about all the rest. We've still got those six thugs out there somewhere. I'm sure their intentions toward us haven't changed."

"I'm agree that they haven't. So we'll have to be very careful from now on. No matter what we do, we'll have to constantly keep our guard up."

"That's okay for the four of us, but it'll be difficult for a lot of the deputies."

"It always is, Lisa, but this time they'll have to listen to us. We'll just have to somehow convince them how serious this situation really is."

"I know we have to do that. But it will be better if we can find those guys before they get to any of us."

"You're right about that. So we have to do everything we can to find them."

CHAPTER 14

The two men stood in the shadows, looking down the long driveway. It was still empty. They should have been there by now. So where were they? They left the bar two hours ago. After their victories over the rather stupid men there, it was a near certainty that they would have come straight here. They were looking for information, they said. So it was only natural that they'd come.

"I don't think they're coming," The man with red hair said. He ran his hand through his hair, which was now beginning to be sprinkled with grey. "This makes no sense. People like them, they always follow through. If they were doing things the way we should be able to expect, they would have come."

"You're right," said the second man. He paused to run his hand over his heavy mustache, which matched the blond hair on his head. "They should have been here by now. It's doubtful they'll come now."

"I guess we might as well tell the others that they can relax."

"Yes, but we still should keep a couple of them on guard. We'll change every four hours. You and I will take the third watch. We'll keep that rotation for a couple of days. Then we might as well go back to the original plan, and kill them one at a time as each opportunity arises."

"Yeah, but it's sure too bad they didn't show up today," he said as he again ran his fingers through his red hair. "It couldn't have been better. Any other day and we wouldn't have been here. All this just happened by accident. They had no way of knowing we were here just to visit the ladies. It would have made for such a great trap."

"It would have been, if they would have come. But don't call what we visited here ladies. Most of them don't rise up that high. Looking at them, it isn't hard to see why they were rejected for shipment, and kept here for the local clients."

"It's true. They ain't here for their looks. But the one I had today, well, let's just say she knew how to satisfy a man."

"Be my guess," the blond commented, "that half the reason you liked her is because your hair's the same color. The same shade even. About the only difference is the parts of grey in yours."

"Don't be knocking my hair. If you'd been doing this job as long as me, you'd be carrying some grey too."

The blond laughed. "True, but on me, it wouldn't show near so much."

The redhead agreed and they went inside to tell the other men about the new plan. Then the two who were to take the first guard duty went to their designated guard stations, and the rest of them looked for someplace to get comfortable.

The redhead looked for the woman he was with when the earlier call came telling them that the police might be on their way. He found her in one of the rooms used to service clients, and was pleased that she was there alone. She smiled when he joined her. It was almost a real smile. Close enough, anyway, to fool the man who joined her in the bed.

She wasn't at all pleased to have him there. In the three months since she was kidnapped and used as a prostitute in this dismal place that was once a country school house, she'd learned to hate all men. This one, with the hair the same color hair as hers, wasn't quite so bad as the others though. At least he didn't have to hit her in order to get aroused.

She sighed heavily when he moved in close to her. She was hoping he would take longer before he needed to do it again. He didn't need more time though, so without any preliminaries, he moved over her. She was pleased when like all the other times he'd used her, it was over quickly. Short time or not, she was quick witted enough to fake a response.

"I like it," he said as he rolled off her, "that you get something out of this too. Most whores don't seem to like it much. Sure, the good ones fake it some. But you…you like it. Makes it better for a man if you like it too."

"If you only knew," she thought, "how I really feel. Most of the time with you or any man, it's all I can do to not puke." She was good though, at playing the game. She knew that pleasing him would keep him there. At least for a while. Then, for a while, no one would be beating on her. So she told him, "I have to make a confession. With the other men I have to be with, I really don't like it much. You though, you are special. Even if I didn't like you, which I do, I think my body would react to you."

"You know what a man wants to hear, don't you?" He laughed, letting her see he was enjoying her. "Truth is, there ain't no way I can believe you or not believe you. I know you'd about say anything to please me, 'cause it's easier for you if you say the right things. I don't care which it is. I just kind of like you. So tell me, where'd you come from?"

She named a small town in the middle of South Dakota. "I'm originally from St. Paul, but my husband's from South Dakota. He owns the grocery store there."

"You grew up in a city, and then you lived in a small town in the middle of nothing and nowhere. I hate places like that. If it was a me, I think I'd find this life right here better than that."

"It doesn't matter now," she said, letting her guard down, by allowing some of her profound sadness show through. "No matter what, I can never go back. My husband is a counsel member of his church. It's a very strict part of the evangelicals. He'll never accept me again. Not after what I've done here."

"If that's true, he ain't much of a husband. If I had a way and a place, I'd keep you. Nothing you've done would stop me neither."

She thought about what he said. Maybe if she tried hard enough, he'd actually take her with him. Anything to escape this horrible place. She'd tried escaping when she was first brought there, but they caught her soon after she got to the end of the driveway. The beating that followed kept her from trying it again.

"I think I'd like it," she told him, "if you took me with you. I'd take care of you, and always be good to you and for you. We're already good together, and I'll bet it would just get better. And I'd always be there, only for you."

He listened to what she said, and gave it some thought. But there was no way he'd ever take her with him. The truth was, he was sure all along that she was faking everything. That was okay, here, in this place. It was just a game that he'd often played with other prostitutes. But now, she'd just carried it too far. Playing that she really cared for him.

When he was young, there was a woman who swore her love for him. Who said that no matter what, she'd always be true to him. He'd returned her love with all his heart and soul. Right up until the day he went to her apartment to surprise her with an engagement ring. He used the key she'd given him to let himself in. The surprise that day was on him. He found her in bed with his best friend. When all was said and done, he killed them both, disappeared and learned his trade. He was a hired killer.

So her claim to always be true to him rang sour. It was something he couldn't in any way believe. If she'd just gone along with what he said by being the good whore she was, everything would have been fine. Making those claims though, about being true, was too much. It destroyed the illusion for him. So it was with a great deal of disgust that he picked up the pillow on his side of the bed.

She didn't see it coming, but she struggled hard to stay alive anyway. It was a struggle she lost. For him, what he did was fully justified. She should never have played that always be true game. There was one other woman he'd been watching who he believed played the game. He simply couldn't believe that a looker like her would ever even want to be true to one man. And the way she played the game with her husband, sickened and angered him.

She was going to be the next lying bitch on his list to kill. All the others would get what they were there to give them. Her and her games were the first on his list. He'd do the job on all of them, but she was the bitch he wanted most to kill. "So, Lisa Thomas," he thought as he walked away from the bed, "you're the next lying bitch who is going to die."

He shuddered then, at the thought of women who claimed to be true to one man. No one in his life had ever been really true.

CHAPTER 15

"**B**ut, Mom," young Sandra Lacey said, "I'm sixteen now. I should be able to go to the mall without you along."

"I don't like the idea of you going to places like that alone," her mom argued. "It's too dangerous for someone as young as you."

"I won't be alone. Jessica is going with me."

"She's no older than you, so going with her isn't much different from going alone."

"Well, I think it is. But even if it isn't, the mall is full of cops. Nothing's going to happen to us with all those cops around."

"I still don't like the idea of you going, even with Jessica. But this time I will let you, *if,* and only if, you go before noon on Saturday. And I want you out of there and back home by no later than five o'clock."

"That's awful early, Mom. Most of our friends get to stay until at least nine."

"I don't care. If you make it any later, you'll be totally grounded for at least a month. It's up to you, my rules or you don't go."

"Your rules I guess, but I just don't see why you always have to be so ridged."

"I'm strict because I love you and I want you to be safe. We live in a mean world, Sandra. A world that *is not safe* for a beautiful girl like you to be out alone in. It's a sad thing, but a true one, that there is a lot of men out there who want nothing so much as taking you and forcing you to do unspeakable things. And they won't hesitate to hurt you to force you to do them."

"People as old as you keep saying stuff like that, but kids my age don't believe it. We all think you keep telling us that just so you can control us."

"I'm glad," Mom said, the tone of her voice showing her impatience with her daughter's attitude, "that you, at your age, know so much more than I do. After all, you're the one with the important life experience. All I've ever done is work full-time since I was seventeen, help put your dad through college, and raise you alone since your dad left us."

"I know all that, but you still should let me stay longer at the mall."

"You're lucky I'm letting you go at all. The hour restrictions will apply no matter how much you argue. And it will take damn little more arguing and you won't be going at all."

Sandra wanted to continue the argument, but knew her mom well enough to know it would be not only futile to continue, but also detrimental to her ability to go at all if she did. So she resigned herself to going to the mall with restricted hours, and spent the rest of the week daydreaming about all the things she hoped to do while she was there.

It seemed like forever for her, but Saturday did finally arrive. She woke up excited, and her excitement only increased as she got ready to go. The one thing she wanted to do while she got dressed, was leave her bra at home. She knew she'd attract more boys without it, but also knew she'd never get past her mother if that's how she dressed.

It seemed to take forever to get ready, but she actually did it with time to spare. She left home when she was ready anyway. Neither she nor her friend Jessica had a car, so they planned to ride the express bus that would take them directly to the mall.

Sandra walked to the designated bus stop for the bus. It was only two blocks from home, so it was a quick walk. She thought about her mother during it, trying to understand why she was always so nervous about simple things like going to the mall. Her mother was so nervous she'd even told Sandra to be careful during the short walk to the bus stop. It was really silly she decided, for her to worry about something so totally safe.

She completely forgot about her mother then, when she arrived at the bus stop and found her friend Jessica already there. They immediately started talking about the things teenage girls talk about, and for the rest of the day enjoyed the freedom gained by being far removed from worried parents.

They were forced to retain the schedule that Sandra was given though. Jessica was given the same schedule. And for Jessica, the schedule was even tougher to break. She had a father at home to assist her mother in enforcing it.

They had the same schedule to start with because Sandra's mother talked often too Jessica's mother. The girls liked, in some ways, the fact that they talked to each other, but hated the fact that it made it difficult to get away with any mischief.

So when the day ended much sooner than they thought it should, the girls reluctantly caught the express bus home. The bus stop appeared empty when they got there. So they felt perfectly safe when they departed the bus with their few packages of things they bought at the mall, and made their goodbyes.

Sandra was the first to learn why her mother constantly worried about her safety. As soon as she left the bus stop, two men jumped out of a white cargo van cruising slowly by, and grabbed her. They covered her mouth before she could scream, and forced her into the van. It quickly turned around and drove off in Jessica's direction. When it caught up with her, they grabbed her the same way.

Her thoughts were the same as Sandra's were when it happened. Mom and Dad were right. It was dangerous to be out alone.

The girls quickly found out how really dangerous it was beyond just being kidnapped. They were quickly stripped and made to lie down on a blanket on the floor at the back of the van. As they lay there, side by side, they were repeatedly raped by the three men in the van. After they'd been riding for a while, the van was stopped and a different man took over the driving. That gave the original driver the chance to rape both the girls.

When the girls were sure it couldn't possibly get worse, the van stopped and they were taken into a building. There, they were pushed into cages, which were actually just large, portable dog kennels.

One of the men who brought them there was talking to someone who was already there. "Yeah," he said, "it's too damn bad if they don't like it that they ain't virgins no more. Me and the boys got tired of gettin' nothing. We're the ones takin' all the chances, grabbing them girls. Not them big shots."

"But they're the ones who pay the big money to us for the girls. You cut the value of those two a lot when you couldn't keep your damn hands off them."

"It don't matter none to me. Them two girls was just too pretty to let them pass us by. Maybe next time you'll get them virgins. This time it was for us. It was good too. So good, we'll likely do 'em again. Couple of real beauties like them two youngsters, and it'd be nuts to not take our share of them."

He was out of luck though. Within a couple of hours, two of the six men who were from Georgia, stopped by to check out the new material they had in stock. Only one more girl was required now to fill the quota for delivery, and they wanted to be sure the new stock made the required quality.

"Yes," said the red haired visitor, "they'll do nicely." Even he was surprised by the beauty of the new girls. He was especially impressed by the one who said her name was Sandra. For one so young, she had a look about her that could do nothing less than arouse him. After watching her for a while, he knew he couldn't leave the place without sampling the goods.

"What kind of money," he asked, "do you need for me to use that one," he pointed at Sandra, "for a full night."

"You ought to know," the man said, "that we aren't allowed to use the girls we keep here that way. You're part of the organization, so you know these girls are for shipment only. No one is allowed to use them. If I let you use her for just a quick one, I could get in serious trouble. If I let you have her all night, they might get angry enough to have me killed."

"The thing is," the redhead said, "I don't care about any of that shit. So you can name the price, or I can put a bullet in your head and use her for nothing."

"I don't think you can just kill me. The company isn't going to let you get away with something like that."

"They don't have much choice. Not many can do what I do as well as I do it. What you do, on the other hand, is pretty simple. Finding someone to replace you is easy. Even a woman could do what you do."

The man knew he was right. All he did is guard and feed the girls waiting for shipment. It didn't take much in the way of brains or skill to do the job. Without more discussion, he opened Sandra's cage.

"I can't charge you," he said. "If I did, the company would think I did this for money." He went into another room.

The redhead gave Sandra some clothes to put on, and after she dressed, took her out of the room they were in, down a hallway, and into a room with a bed. There, he undressed her again. She whimpered the whole time. He didn't know that the men who kidnapped her, along with the men who worked at this facility, had already used her many times over. He was expecting a virgin.

"This won't take long," he told her. "You being who you are, will do it for me the way those used up whores can't."

He dropped his pants around his ankles, then crawled on top of her on the bed. His plan was to take her as quickly as he could. He loved the way virgins squirmed and cried when he took them, when he took what they considered their own treasure. At this stage of their lives, they all seemed to think it was something to be saved for just the right man.

He smiled at his last thought. He might not be their *right* man, but he was damn sure *the* man. Anxious now, he quickly forced himself on her. He was inside her as deep as he could go, before he realized there hadn't been any resistance. He pulled out of her, moved back, and stared at her, His face was filled with disgust.

"You little whore," he growled with clenched teeth. "You damn little whore. You been doing it already. You shouldn't of never done that. You was supposed to save it for me."

He hit her with an open hand, swinging it back and forth across her face. She screamed in terror and pain. That angered him more, so he balled up both fists and started to pummel her with them. Her face, head, and entire body were his targets. It didn't matter now, how much he hit her, it didn't abate his anger. She cheated on him when she did it.

She wasn't supposed to do anything with anyone before him. In his anger, it never occurred to him that she had nothing to do with the fact she was no longer a virgin. She lost it by force. She was raped. If he would have asked her, she could have told him. Then he could have taken out his anger on the right people.

It was too late now though. She was beaten senseless. Her body and face were bloody and broken. Her breathing was already shallow, coming in fits and starts. As his beating slowed and finally stopped, he realized that she had little chance of making it. As he watched her labored breathing, he wondered to himself, why no woman on earth was ever loyal. All this one had to do is wait a while. It would have been fine for the two of them if she'd just waited.

She didn't though, and like all the other times they'd cheated, or lied about being true and faithful, it was too late for this one. Finally, he couldn't stand to look at her any longer. She cheated on him, and now deserved the ultimate.

After one last look at her now ugly, battered face, he moved a pillow over her head. Because of her condition, it didn't take long for him to accomplish his mission.

He wrapped her in the blanket that covered the bed and carried her out to his car. This time, he was going to use her to send a message. He didn't have to go far to do it.

He'd never done it before, but this time he could warn, and preferably scare, four future targets. Four people he now hated. They were no longer just people he needed to kill. Killing them now was personal. The were the ultimate, all of them. Wives pretending to be true to their husbands. Husbands pretending to be true to their wives. Women never were, and men rarely were. The ones he hated the most are the ones who were the best at pretending. He thought about them one at a time, beginning with the one he hated most. After having watched her for a while now, he understood why Sheriff Tod Mcintire hated her so much. She was always playing at being so in love with her husband. Her husband, Mack, all too often played the same game. They'd been married long enough. He should be tired of her by now.

As far as he was concerned, Lisa Thomas was the best, and the worst, example of an untrue, cheating wife. No woman who looked like her could ever remain true. It made no sense for her to do it. Looks like hers, she could have about any man she ever wanted.

The other three weren't quite so evil, but they tended to pretend to care more about their men than what, in truth, women really ever did. Two of them anyway. Wanda Thomas and Theresa Thomas. The fourth in the bunch lived alone, that was true. But her home was part of the ranch they owned, and he was sure she must be cheating with all three of the married men. That meant Sue Sartor was also on his list of targets. Just on general principles. He and the other five were there to kill everyone giving the company trouble. So he would kill them. And enjoy doing it.

He wanted what he was doing this night, to tell that whole bunch that their time was about up. Soon, he and the five men he'd come to this place called Clayborne County with, would eliminate them. And in doing it, he was determined to be the one to kill Lisa. In all the years he'd been eliminating enemies of the company, he'd never cared about who, why, or when. He just did the job. This time though, there'd be at least one exception.

He needed to be careful though. In his profession, he wasn't allowed to feel anything about the targets. So if he let it show to anyone that he felt the way he did, he would at least be sent back to Georgia. If he caused much concern with the top people of the company, he'd end up the same way his targets did. Dead. Very dead.

That was his last thought about anything but what he was now doing. He killed the car lights as he got close, and stopped near the driveway. He knew better than to make any noise. The Thomas's reputation had grown over the years, and was known far and wide by the criminal element. So it was with care that he took Sandra Lacey's body out of his car, and laid it down into the ditch next to the driveway.

"That ought to tell them people something come morning," he thought as he drove away. He felt good now. He was sure that what he did was going to put the fear of God in them. Not to mention the fear of what was going to happen to them.

Had he actually known or understood the hated Thomas family, he might have understood what a gross mistake he'd just made. That, however, was something men like him rarely, if ever, did.

CHAPTER 16

After they were all there, with their full breakfast plates in front of them, Ben remembered the question he wanted to ask. "Did anyone else hear anything around midnight last night? I'm not sure, but I could have sworn I heard a car door close, then a car drive off."

None of them had, not even Theresa, his wife. But since she was in bed next to him at the time, she asked him, "were you awake when you heard it, or did it wake you up?"

Ben shook his head, trying to remember. "You know," he answered her, "I'm not really sure. But I don't remember laying awake, so the sound probably woke me up."

"Do you think the sound could have been part of a dream that woke you up?"

"Could have been I guess. But I don't remember any dream, so I don't think so. I'm usually one of those who remembers the dreams that wake me up."

"Either way, it was probably nothing," Roy said.

Roy's wife, Wanda, voiced her own opinion. "Don't be so sure, Roy," she said. "Dreams can mean a lot, as you should all know. Even though it looks like Mack and I might be finally shed of the ones we used to have, that doesn't mean other dreams can't mean something."

Lisa suddenly dropped her fork and started shaking. She had been the last person to benefit directly from the warning dreams Mack and

Wanda used to have. Those dreams saved her life. Now something like them seemed to be affecting her. Because of the conversation they all believed it was Ben's dream doing it. At least the talk of it was doing something to Lisa.

Mack took her shaking hand and gave it a light squeeze. "Are you okay?" She didn't answer right away, so he held her hand until it stopped shaking. She took a few deep breaths when it did, then said, "I don't think it was a dream. Somethings wrong. Something bad's happened. Ben heard part of it."

She got up then, and hurried outside. Mack and Wanda followed her to the end of the driveway. She was in the ditch when they caught up with her. She was struggling to open a rolled up blanket.

Even before she had it opened enough to see what was inside, she said, "Someone's going to pay for this. Someone's going to definitely pay."

What they saw when she got the blanket open was horrifying. The open eyes set deep in their sockets, stared up at them from Sandra's mutilated face. Lisa dropped her head, shaking it as she looked at the crime that was once Sandra. Mack put his arm around Wanda and pulled her close. He could feel the anger build inside her as they stood there, unable for the moment to do anything else.

What they were seeing was as terrible a thing to look at as anything any of them had ever seen.

It didn't take long for the rest of the family to realize something was wrong, and leave the house to join them by the ditch.

"This isn't something any of you want to see," Mack told them before they got too close. Sue had her cell phone in her hand, so he told her, "Call 911. Tell them there's been a murder and where we are. Then let me use your phone. When she finished her call, she gave the phone to Mack. He called Dale.

Roy reached for Wanda's hand, and held it while she left the ditch. They stood next to Ben and Theresa. Both women had tears in their eyes as they watched Mack move the blanket over Sandra's face, then wrap his arm around Lisa and walk her out of the ditch.

She wasn't crying. Not only was anger written all over her face, she was so stiff with it throughout her body that her movements were stilted. Mack just held her, knowing it would take some time for her to get passed this. She, more than any of them, related to what kind of hell Sandra went through before she died.

Whatever it was that the person who did this thought they were proving by dumping Sandra's body there, was wrong. All they accomplished was to make everyone there totally dedicated to stopping whoever was responsible. Not only for this travesty, but for all of them that were in any way connected to this kind of crime.

As Lisa calmed, she leaned hard against Mack. She knew he understood when she looked up to him and said, "This is going to stop. Maybe not everywhere, but at least anywhere we can do something about it. And the men who do this. They have to pay. One way or the other, they have to pay."

Mack didn't argue with her or tell her to calm down or do any of the usual things normally done with someone who had Lisa's determined attitude. He couldn't. He agreed with her. Someone had to pay. Someone was going to pay. It didn't matter now what it might take. They were, one way or the other, going to pay.

The place where Sandra was dropped soon became a place filled with the crime scene people. As experienced as they were, they were to a person, sickened by what they were forced to deal with.

After a while, the team's leader brought Dale, Paul, Mack, and Lisa together. "I don't have much new to tell you about what happened to that young lady. She was murdered. I know it appears that she was beaten to death, but the beating didn't kill her. She was suffocated. The beating would have killed her eventually, but apparently whoever did this didn't want to wait."

"Will you be able to check the murderers DNA?" Dale asked him.

"Probably. It'll take some time to isolate it, but I'm sure we'll end up with it. But there's one thing the killer won't be able to hide for quite sometime. I'm sure he used his fists to beat her. There's no way he could do to her what he did without doing serious damage to those fists. You want to find the man who did this, find the one with the mangled hands, and you'll have him."

"We'll find him," Lisa said. "One way or the other, we'll find him."

Everyone in the Clayborne County Sheriff's Department, from Sheriff Dale Magee on down, wanted to be involved in this investigation. Only a few actually saw the body of Sandra Lacey, but somehow a description of the way it looked quickly spread throughout the department. It made what happened to her seem personal to each and every member of the department. It was a feeling they all normally tried to avoid. It wasn't good to take things personal. But this time, it seemed impossible not to. What was done to her went beyond anything that could be taken anyway but personal.

After Sandra's body was removed from the ditch and taken to the morgue, Dale called the pathologist who would be performing the autopsy and requested it be given a priority. He also requested that the people who would be checking her DNA to do the same.

He knew that identifying her would help with the investigation. For now, they didn't have any idea of who she was. That meant they didn't have any idea where she lived or where she was or what she was doing before she was murdered.

The only solid lead they had to go on was the fact that the body was dumped where it was. It seemed a stretch that it was simply a random act, done by a random individual. Especially not so soon after Mack and Lisa they did what they did in the bar in the town of Baptism Towers.

It was known by the criminals involved that they were actively investigating the human trafficking going on in that part of Minnesota. They were already expecting some kind of retaliation from those people, given there were six killers, somewhere near, already planning to kill them. So they couldn't help wonder if the battered body in the ditch might be some kind of warning or threat to scare them off their investigation. If it was, it was a stupid thing to do. Now, more than ever before, they were determined to do whatever they could to capture those responsible for this particularly vicious murder.

There was little they could immediately do though, so everyone went back to their normal duties. Mack was driving through the townhouse/condo area of the Lands Magnificent resort when he got a call on the police radio. Something he rarely got now, in the era of the cell phone. The call was about a domestic disturbance in one of the townhouses. A woman had called, saying she was afraid her husband would kill her. Mack did a U-turn and drove the two blocks back to the townhouse.

A man and a woman were out in front of it. He held her by her wrist and had something in his other hand he was shaking it in front of her face. Mack couldn't be sure what it was, so he unhooked the loop holding his gun in place in his shoulder holster.

"What seems to be the problem?" he asked as he approached the couple. As he got close, he could see that the object in the man's hand was a cell phone.

The man let go of her wrist, quickly slapped the woman hard across the face, and grabbed her wrist again. He then turned to Mack. "This isn't anything for you to be concerned with, cowboy. So it will be best for your health if you just get back in the truck of your's, and get the hell out of here."

Mack pointed to the badge hooked to his belt and said, "I'm here because of a domestic disturbance call. I just saw you hit her, so now I'm assuming that you are the disturbance."

"Don't matter. It's still none of your concern. This is just me and the wife having a disagreement. There's nothing you can do about that."

Along with keeping an eye on the man, Mack was also looking at the woman. She had multiple bruises on her face and arms. He could only guess what she had on the areas of her body he couldn't see.

"It's like this," he said. "I did see you hit her. She's covered with bruises, which I can only assume that you inflicted on her. So I'm not about to walk away and let you continue to hurt her."

"You can't prove I did anything to her, so you can't tell me what to do or make me do anything."

"Truth is," Mack said, "I can prove it, so there's plenty I can do about it. So let her go. Now!"

"If you were smart, cowboy, you'd turn yourself around and get the hell out of here. You don't, and you will regret it."

"Was that a threat?"

"Call it what you want."

"I call it physical abuse, so since you're not at all cooperating, I'm placing you under arrest for assault."

"Please don't do that," the woman pleaded, her eyes filled with terror as she faced Mack. "You'll just make things worse."

"Shut the hell up," the man yelled as he shoved the cell phone into his back pocket. He slapped her again twice, first with his hand, then the back of his hand.

That was enough for Mack. He pushed the man away from the woman, then stepped between them. The man took a quick swing at Mack. He easily moved out of the way, and grabbed the man's arm. He gave it a quick twist, and threw the man to the ground. He dropped down on him, his knee on the man's back. In seconds, Mack had him cuffed.

"Please," the woman continued to plead, "don't arrest him. He'll just blame me if you do."

"He can't," Mack told her. "I'm not going to charge him with assaulting you. He assaulted me. That carries a heavier penalty than assaulting you does. At minimum, his activities today are going to cost him some jail time, or at least a fair amount of money."

"I'm going to have you crucified for this," the man threatened. "You are done with pulling this kind of crap. I'll have your badge before the day is over." He looked at the woman. "And you bitch, you're going to pay dearly for this. You shouldn't of made that call."

"Now look what you've done," the woman said to Mack. "You've just made it worse for me."

"If you're that afraid," Mack told her, "I can take you somewhere safe."

"No, no you can't. He'll find me. He always finds me."

"I don't think it's a good idea for you to stay here."

"I have too. I don't have anywhere else to go."

Mack was becoming frustrated with her. He was in the middle of an all too familiar situation, but one he had no patience for. He knew how difficult it was for her, dealing with an abusive man like this, but also felt she should be willing to try do something about it. If she wasn't, there was little he could do about it.

He brought the man to the station, locked him up, did the paperwork, down loaded the episode from his body camera, and then left. When he got to his truck, he called Lisa on his cell phone, told her what happened, and asked her to do at least a drive-by of the townhouse at the end of her shift. He knew how things like this went, and had little doubt the man would be out on bail in a matter of hours.

The rest of the day went by with relatively little going on. Even so, when it was over it seemed as though the whole department gave it a collective sigh of relief.

Mack and Lisa were especially glad to have it over. After the discovery of the body in the ditch in the morning, it was the kind of day they just wanted to forget. So with her thoughts on other things, Lisa was nearly halfway home before she remembered Mack's request that she check on the domestic abuse victim he'd dealt with in the morning.

Thinking she'd be able to get by with just driving by the place, she was shocked by what she saw. The woman was laying in her back on the sidewalk in front of the place, obviously helpless to move. The man was standing over her, staring down on her. When Lisa got out of her pickup and closed the door, the man looked at her, then kicked the woman on the ground hard.

"Stop that now," Lisa yelled.

He kicked her again. Lisa moved in and pushed him away. He instantly took a swing at her. The blow came too fast for her to get completely out of the way, but she managed to deflect most of its force. He tried again, but this time missed completely.

"Stand still you damn bitch," he screamed. "I'm going to kill you. You damn cops got no right to be here." He threw another feeble punch.

Like it was earlier for Mack, watching someone beat up a woman after seeing the body they saw in the morning, it was too much. But unlike Mack, Lisa decided arresting this individual just didn't seem to be the right thing to do. He'd already been arrested, and now here he was, beating this woman senseless. So she decided to let him dig his own grave. She again pushed him away. Knowing what his response would be, she was ready for him. she countered his wild swing with the palm of her right hand. It landed perfectly, with all the force she could give it, on his nose. She knew from the sound and the way it felt, that she broke it.

She stepped back, waiting for him to see the blood pouring from it. As she knew he would, he charged her. It was what she wanted. She easily sidestepped him, used her foot to trip him, and slammed the side of her fist onto the back of his head on his way down. She didn't hit him hard enough to knock him out. She wanted him to get back up one more time.

He did, and again charged her. This time she stepped inside his blows, and landed several hard punches to his stomach. as he doubled over, she brought her knee up into his already bloody face. She then pushed him and as he staggered back, she kicked him with everything she could put together. She felt the toe of her boot go deep as it landed with a perfect strike between his legs. She couldn't be sure she did any permanent damage to him. She could only hope.

She called for an ambulance, then for backup. Dale and two deputies were already there when Mack arrived. The ambulance was loading the woman and one of ambulance people was looking at the man, who was on the ground, moaning loudly. He was holding on tightly between his legs and wouldn't allow anyone to look at that part of his body. Lisa was watching him, struggling to hide the grin that was trying to fill her face.

All Mack said when he walked up to her was, "I hope you had your camera on."

"I did."

"And he took the first swing?"

"Four of them first. All I did was try to get him away from the woman."

"Good. Maybe it'll stick when we both press charges."

"Well, Mack, if it doesn't, maybe I can convince him to attack me again." She snickered.

CHAPTER 17

Mack knew it was time to check out the house they'd learned about at the Old Time Inn, in Baptism Towers. Having the badly beaten body of Sandra Lacey dumped in the ditch next to their driveway was more than he could let slide by. Something had to be done, and the house up there in Jackstone County was the best lead they had on what was going on, so it was the best place to make the next move.

He didn't as yet want to involve most of the department, so he asked Lisa and Paul to join him and Dale during their next coffee break. When they joined Dale and Mack, Dale wasn't surprised, even though he didn't know they were coming. After viewing Sandra Lacey's body the previous day, he'd expected Mack to do something.

When they finished their usual hellos and good mornings, without any more preliminaries, Dale said, "So, what's the plan, Mack?"

"It's time to check out the house up in Jackstone County."

"When do you plan on doing it? Today?"

"No, Dale," Mack explained. "The timing would be wrong. I want to do it tomorrow morning, early."

"How early?"

"Four-thirty is the time I want to check them out. Everyone should be sleeping then, so there'll be less chance of any of them getting away. If we get lucky, we might even catch the hired guns there."

"That would be lucky," Dale agreed, "because they'd be awful stupid to stay in such a rather public type place."

"I know. What I'm really hoping, is that someone in that house will know where they hang out, and we can go after them even before we finish up with the house."

"That's going to take a lot of deputies. How many are you planning to take along on this raid?"

"Every deputy not on the day shift."

"How can you do that, and still make the raid at four-thirty in the morning?"

"Easy. Have the day shift start early. If the county objects to the overtime next payday, Lisa and I will cover it."

"I'm getting more than a little tired of you two covering things like this. This is some real serious crime we're dealing with here. The county should pay for it. I'll do everything I can to force them to do it."

"Don't worry about it, Dale. We both know that's not going to happen as long as people continue to elect conservative commissioners. They're not about to spend money on crime, when they can use the county money for projects they and other wealthy people can profit from."

Lisa, who along with Paul had been silent this whole time, interrupted them. "I know," she said, "that if we could fix the politics, we could fix a lot of the problems. But we can't. The general public will have to do that, and we all know how unlikely it is that that will happen. So let's talk more about what we're going to do tomorrow. But before we do that, Do you know, Dale, who the girl was who was dumped in our ditch yesterday?"

"Yes. I got that report shortly after I got to the office this morning. Her name was Sandra Lacey. She, along with a friend of hers who is still missing, was kidnapped when they went to the mall the day before yesterday. We're still not absolutely sure, but we think the two girls were taken after they got off the express bus near their home."

"Has anyone talked to the parents yet?" Paul asked. "Sometimes they can help piece together what happened."

"The Minneapolis Police have. That's why we know the little we know. We hope to learn more later. For now, they're too upset to tell us much."

"I'm surprised they could tell you anything," Lisa said. "If something like that happened to a kid of mine, I doubt I could function at all. That's another reason we've got to do something to stop the traffickers. Doing what they're doing is hurting way too many people. Something else we all definitely need to realize. The people involved in trafficking, no matter what the level of their involvement, have not one thing positive to offer any part of the human race or anything else. They should be treated accordingly."

"We all agree with you on that, Lisa," Mack told her. "So let's do more than something. Let's raise all the hell with them as is humanly possible."

"That's exactly what we need to do, Mack," Paul said. "So give us your plan as to how we're going to do it."

He did, and it extended their coffee break well beyond its normal time. But they were all primed for the next days action when they left Katy's and moved into their normal day's work. Only Dale had a significant day. Group by group, he brought deputies into the sheriff's office conference room and explained what their duties would be during the following day's action. By the end of the day, the entire Clayborne County Sheriff's Department was primed and ready to take on the world of human trafficking.

Later that same day, that same world was planning its own assault on the Clayborne County Sheriff's Department, starting with Mack and Lisa Thomas.

"We should take out the sheriff next," suggested ex-sheriff Tod Mcintire.

"I agree," said the redheaded Jocko Mason. "His wife too. She thinks she's the queen of the world, now that she's some kind of big time singer. Be my guess, she's screwing around on him too. The damn bitch. *Yes!* We for sure got to do her too."

"You sure got a hard against women, don't you Jocko," one of the six men in the bunker said.

"You might say that," he agreed. "But only them cheating kind. Those what stay true, no, I ain't got nothing against them."

"Since I ain't ever seen you like one yet, them true kind must be few and far between."

"They are. Almost no one is. Man or women. But women who aren't, well, they're much worse than men who aren't. For men, it's their nature to move around from one woman to another. For women, it's because they're evil cheaters. Lisa Thomas and the sheriff's wife, Kathy Magee, are the worst of the worst. Both pretend to be so true. Both aren't. A woman can't look like they do, and stay true. It just ain't possible. I'm gonna have me a taste of both of them anyway. Just before we kill the bitches."

Having moved across the room from Jocko, ex-sheriff Tod Mcintire said to the man next to him, "He is one hard ass bastard, ain't he?"

"He for sure is. And he ain't one too screw with neither. So it'd be best you watch what you say. You say something he don't like, and one way or the other, he will get you for it."

The ex-sheriff was just smart enough to listen, and made it a point to stay away from Jocko the rest of the evening. He did, however, listen closely to Jocko's plan for the large amount of killing they were sent to Clayborne County to commit. Killing which was to start the following evening, right after the day shift ended at the Clayborne County sheriff's department.

When they finished going over their plans, it was late into the night. Only two short hours before Mack and Lisa were getting out of bed. They were up early enough to have time for showers before they got dressed. But they ran into trouble when Mack decided it would be fun to shower with Lisa. By the time they finished, they were running a bit late, and were a few minutes late to meet the rest of the group who were part of their mission.

It was two groups actually. The first group would be invading the house where the working prostitutes were. The second group would be used only if they got enough information about the location of the six killers to go after them.

Four members of the team would be part of both raids, if there were more than one. Dale, being the sheriff, would of course be the lead of both actions. The other three were Mack, Lisa, and Paul.

They traveled north to Jackstone County in several vehicles, with Mack and Lisa in Mack's large pickup in the lead. Dale and Paul followed in the sheriff's car, with the rest in order by group.

To avoid detection, they left the highway before they reached Baptism Towers, and carefully moved along various country backroads without lights. They made it to the house without any problems, and were lucky to find an out of sight alfalfa field close by the house to park in.

The house was dark, and it appeared that everyone inside was sleeping. They'd had their usual late night activities, and were naturally tired, except of course, those who were passed out from drugs or alcohol.

Mack led the first group of deputes to the house, which they surrounded. They wanted to be sure that when they broke in, no one would escape by jumping out a window.

The house had three doors. A front and back door into the house itself, and an old-fashioned cellar door. They decided to leave the invasion of the cellar until after they had control of the house. Two deputies stood guard on it while the they moved on the house.

Mack was the first in. He used the front door. Lisa was right behind him. A guard was stationed there, sitting in an overstuffed chair. Rather than actually doing any guarding, however, he was busy with a somewhat battered young lady when they got inside.

He was holding tightly to her hair, forcing the young lady to perform oral sex on him. The shock of seeing Mack and Lisa, followed by several other deputies, made him jump from the chair. Unfortunately for him, the young lady being forced didn't react as quickly or the same. Instead of letting him go, she bit down hard with her young, sharp teeth. He screamed and she spit out the sudden flow of blood.

The invaders had hoped to keep things quiet until deputies managed to infiltrate most of the building. The man's scream destroyed that, but to stop him from making any more noise, Mack quickly dispatched him with a heavy blow to the back of his head with his gun. The man fell hard, and lay there bleeding profusely where he was bitten.

Mack and Lisa left him and moved farther into the house. The building they were in was originally a bed and breakfast. It drew people to stay there by presenting itself as a taste of life on an old-fashioned farm. Of course, the only taste of that life style that guests ever got was the food. Any of the rest of farm life in the old days would have proved to be too much work and too difficult for anyone's liking.

The place went out of business several years ago, and sat empty for most of those years. It was finally purchased by the local bank. They then leased it to Sheriff Mcintire. He promised to restore it, and turn it into a resort. Which he did, if you can call a whore house with steel interior doors to keep the women working there locked up a resort.

Those doors were enough to keep the women locked up when they weren't working, but did little to keep the Clayborne County deputies out. The door jams were still wood, and gave way easily to them.

As they broke down the doors, they found most of the woman alone. The few that weren't, were anything but upset when the men with them were removed.

To everyone's surprise, the operation went down without any shooting. There were a few rather feeble attempts to stop the deputies from breaking open doors, but they were mostly an irritation. The men who lived and worked there were not in any kind of decent physical condition.

As soon as the search of the main building was complete, Mack, Lisa, Dale, and Paul checked out the cellar. The scene they found there was both tragic and horrifying. Several women were tied to flimsy cots. All were badly beaten, with two of them so battered they were near death. Dale immediately called 911 for ambulances. After a detailed explanation of who he was and what the problem was, three were sent to them.

Lisa and one other female deputy waited with the battered women for the ambulances. Mack, Dale, and Paul went back into the main building to question the captured men who were running the place. They split the questioning into three rooms, and constantly rotated the men from one room to the other. Since each of them, Mack, Dale, and Paul had somewhat different techniques when they questions someone, the men being questioned were kept off balance, and had an ever more hard time remembering their lies or which interrogator they told them to.

About an hour into the questioning, one of the men finally folded, and told Paul the location of the six hired killers, who were planning on wiping out as much of the Clayborne County Sheriff's Department as possible.

Knowing that the longer they waited to go after the men, because of the chance they might hear about the raid on this house, the more dangerous it would get. So they moved to get ready for the second raid.

All the women from the cellar were already on their way to the hospital, with two deputies on their way there too. The other women were now properly dressed, and were ready to be transported to Kingsburg. There was no way they would be turned over to anyone from Jackstone county. All of the women had already said they were initially kidnapped. The state police were now there, and were taking control over the men running the house.

With things mostly under as good of a control as could be expected, the second Clayborne County Sheriff's Department group left the scene for the hideout of the six hired killers. Everyone in this group knew that this time, they'd be facing extremely strong resistance from professionals, who were experts at using weapons of all kinds. The only exception to that was the ex-sheriff Tod Mcintire. He was, at best, adequate with a pistol.

Everyone in the group wore body armor, and to a person they were grateful that what they wore was of the highest quality money could buy. They all were reasonably sure that none of the killers would be wearing any. Unless, of course, they learned that they were about to be raided.

They hadn't though, because no one from the home ever got the chance to warn them, and because the Clayborne County raiders were wise enough to not trust or inform anyone from Jackstone County law enforcement about what they were doing. They didn't even tell the state police of their plans to raid the killers. They all knew that as much as the state police might want to assist them, they would likely get in the way more than help.

As they did at the house, they found a place to leave the vehicles and moved on foot up to the bunker the killers were staying in. From the outside, it appeared to be an old, abandoned shed. But inside the shed, was another structure with a steel door which opened to stairs which went down to the bunker itself.

When they got to the door, it was an instant concern. It was the only apparent entrance to the bunker they could find, and forcing it open would destroy any chance of invading the place by surprise.

It stalled the attack for a few moments, until Mack decided they should break it open, and move as fast as possible into the place. He volunteered, over Lisa's objection, to go through the door first. Just before they started to pry the door open, he checked the door. He was caught by surprise when it opened. Someone forgot to lock it. Both the dead bolt and the door handle were unlocked.

Surprised or not, the instant it opened, he started down the steps. The bunker itself was well built, and the wood steps he went down were a full three feet wide and twelve inches deep. The treads were double two by six, built the same as an outdoor deck would be. There were even railings on both side of the staircase for safety. This allowed Mack to move rapidly, yet still quietly, down the steps. The door at the bottom of the stairs was already open.

At the bottom of them, Mack stepped into a kitchen. Two men who were supposed to be guards were sitting at a kitchen table. Their weapons were on the table, and both men were having trouble keeping their eyes open. But they were awake just enough to hear Mack before he could cross the room and disarm them. They both reached for their guns. When they lifted them to shoot Mack, he had no choice but to fire first. His aim was accurate and the two men died in their chairs.

By this time several deputies, led by Dale, Paul, and Lisa were in the kitchen. As expected, several occupants of the bunker were now also awake. All them were armed, and they quickly readied themselves for the coming battle.

Mack, along with the other three leaders, and a couple of other deputies quickly moved into the next room, which was a community room of sorts. They fanned out, with three of them going down each of the hallways connected to the room. The rest stayed in the main room.

No one got far. Men poured out of the rooms located down each hallway. No one from the sheriff's department hesitated. Anyone with a weapon who was perceived to be a threat was shot. When one of the killers moved out into the hallway using a young girl as a shield, everyone hesitated to shoot. Everyone but Lisa. Steadying herself, she took careful aim at the space barely two inches from the girls head. It only took a moment for the killer to peek out that side of the girl's head to check on what the deputies were doing.

It was all Lisa needed. She fired. Her bullet made a neat little hole in the killers forehead. The girl screamed and as the man dropped to the floor, she ran to Lisa. She wrapped her arms around her as the girl started to cry, with deep, heavy sobs. She began shaking as Lisa held her.

"There's more of us," she said in a trembling voice, "there's more girls. You should help them."

"We will," Lisa assured her. "But first, we've got to get you out of here." She motioned for one of the other deputies to take the girl. As he did, Lisa said, "Get her the complete hell out of this place. Do it now." He did.

The shooting had stopped by then, but it wasn't over. All the rooms needed to be checked. They all knew that doing so was going to be another dangerous proposition. At his own insistence, Mack took the first room. It was empty.

Dale went in first on the second room. The second he stepped into the room a shot rang out. The bullet hit him in the chest. He went down hard, gasping for breath, the wind knocked out of him. His body armor had done its job and saved his life. Paul was right behind him, and shot the killer. He wasn't wearing any armor and died on the spot.

When they were passed the halfway point with the rooms, Lisa went in first. The room appeared empty, but she heard the sound of breathing. It only lasted a few seconds, but it was enough. Since there was nothing in the room other than a small dresser, the bed, and hooks on the wall to hang clothes and things on, she knew the sound had to come from under the bed. Mack was behind her, and she motioned for him to move the bed.

He flipped the entire bed over. Lying there, curled up, was ex-sheriff Tod Mcintire. She looked at him for a few moments. The feelings of contempt she felt toward him filling her.

"Get up, you coward!" she said. He didn't move. She nudged him with her boot. "Get the hell up," she said again. He didn't move. She shook her head. "The hell with it."

The position he was in, left certain body parts vulnerable to attack from the rear. She looked at Mack as she pointed out that fact. He just shrugged. She reared back and kicked him in that spot with everything she had in her. Her pointed toe, western style boot went in deep. He screamed. She gave him a couple of minutes, then again said, "Get up."

He took him a while, but he finally did. He was cuffed and tied to one of the kitchen chairs. The deputy guarding him was told to kill him if he made the slightest move to escape. He didn't make any unnecessary moves that would make the deputy nervous. No moves at all until they came back for him later.

As badly bruised and sore as he was, Dale managed to be the first in the last room. It was the largest room located in the hallway area of the bunker. The door was closed, and when he opened it and charged in there, what he found shocked him. The room was divided into what looked like jail cells, only smaller. There were six of them, and five of them each held a young girl. The cells were high enough to stand in, but there was no cot to sleep on, If the girls wanted to rest or sleep, they had to do it on the floor. Their toilet facilities were five gallon buckets.

All the locks for the cells used the same key, which was hanging on the wall not far from the cells. Lisa got the honor of opening each cell. As she did, every girl gave her a hug when they stepped out of their cage. All but one of them cried at that point.

The one who didn't said, "If you guys will give me a gun I will kill everyone one of those men who are still alive for you."

"You don't really want to do that," Paul said to her.

"Sure she does," Lisa answered for her. "And there is no way you can blame her for it. Everyone of those bastards deserves to die."

Dale, who had just checked on the status of everyone involved in the fight joined them. "It's too late for either one of you to do it. All but two of them are already dead. The ex-sheriff and the guy with the busted up hands. We've got him tied to a chair by the once was sheriff."

"He's the one who killed Sandra Lacey," Lisa said. "Are you sure you won't let me kill him? Maybe at least have some fun cutting him up some?"

"Not this time, Lisa."

The girl who volunteered to do the killing eased her way toward the doorway of the room. Just before she reached it, she managed to get her hands on the holstered weapon of a deputy standing there. She yanked it loose from the holster and took off running down the hall. Lisa, Mack, and Dale caught up with her in the kitchen. She was standing next to the redhead, holding the gun with the barrel inside his mouth.

"You always wanted me to suck on it, you son of a bitch," she told him, her voice a deep growl. "Well now, you can suck on this for a while before I blow you away."

Her right hand was white from gripping the gun so hard. But not as white as the redhead's face. His eyes were now bulging and filled with fear. She jammed the gun further down his throat and he wet his pants.

Not wanting to do anything that might convince the girl to fire, the three of them stood quietly. They didn't want to prevent a shooting for any concern about what happened to the redhead killer. Their only concern was for the girl. They didn't want her to end up in prison for the likes of him. He just wasn't worth it.

The girl then began to realize the same thing. Her grip on the gun eased up and some color returned to her hand. As she seemed to relax, she shook her head a couple of times. At about the same time the three were sure the crisis was over, the girl suddenly ripped the gun out of his mouth. She let her arm fly back behind her head, then brought it back crashing down on the redheaded killer's mouth. It smashed his front teeth, both the uppers and the lowers. His mouth started to bleed and he shit his pants.

The girl dropped the gun on the floor and started to cry. Lisa did everything she could to try to comfort her. While she did, Mack turned to Dale, knowing what he would think they should do to the girl.

"We aren't going to do anything to her," Mack told him, while he pointed at the girl. "No arrest, no pressing charges, no nothing. What she did to him was nothing compared to what he did to her and countless other girls. He tried to escape and was hurt when we were forced to subdue him."

Dale didn't bother to even look at Mack. "I guess I shouldn't have hit him so hard with my gun," he said to no one directly, "but he was trying to kill me."

The only response he got was from Lisa. "You are a damn good man, Sheriff Dale Magee. An outstanding man."

Lisa and Dale gathered all the girls together, and questioned them about any injuries they might have. When none of them complained of any serious enough to need immediate attention, Dale called for transportation to carry them to Kingsburg and safety. Paul Danielson, along with two the deputies rode with them.

As soon as the girls were safely on their way, Mack separated the ex-sheriff and the redheaded killer. Because the redhead was having a great deal of difficulty speaking, he started questioning Tod Mcintire, the ex-sheriff first. As was normal for most hard core criminals, he refused to answer any questions. It didn't take Mack long to know he needed to change his tactics.

He smiled. "Okay," he told Tod, "you don't have to talk to me if you don't want to. But I do need answers to my questions. So what I'm going to do, is leave you alone with Lisa, and let her use whatever methods she chooses to get some answers. All you have to bear in mind now, is the simple truth that you will most likely be missing some body parts before she finishes with you. I think you know which parts I'm referring too."

Tod didn't need anymore convincing. As soon as Lisa joined them, he started answering all the questions he was asked. Quickly, they knew who supplied the killers, and who was the buyer for the girls. As was already suspected, they were one and the same. It was a mafia family, living in Georgia. Mack wrote the information down, on the chance he might need it someday.

Once they got all the information they could get out of their prisoners, they called the state police and let them take charge. This time, the state people relented and let all the Clayborne County people leave after minimal questioning.

It was with a great relief that they all headed for home with all of them still intact. The only wounds they suffered were Dale and one of the deputies being shot. Both were wearing armor, so the damage was limited to serious bruises they would live with for a few days.

CHAPTER 18

For the next few days, Kingsburg witnessed scene after scene of pure joy as girls and women we reunited with their families. Sometimes it was a single mother or father. More often it was both parents. And for several of the girls, it was entire families who came.

Even though everyone connected with the raids and rescues thought it best to avoid any publicity, the local paper quickly learned about what was happening. From there, the story blossomed into a statewide phenomenon.

The sheriff's department did its best to protect the girls and their families, but reporters managed to get stories for the media anyway. As much as they tried, members of the department also tried to avoid becoming a news item.

It did little good though. Sooner or later, many of the deputies involved in the raids were cornered and questioned. Because the stories contained killing, mayhem, and violence in general, they ran for several days in all the media, be it the normal kind or online.

As the stories unfolded a pattern developed. One that neither Mack nor Lisa wanted. It quickly became evident that true or not, they were often part of them, if not an out and out feature in them.

It was then that the worst that could happen with the media happened. Some of the most outrageous stories about them went national. It got so bad for three days that they gave up and stayed home, with the doors locked. The only saving grace was that they spent a lot of that time in bed. Another good thing was the fact that their relationship was such that the time spent inside their house, never at any time got boring.

By evening of the third day, the media finally gave up on getting them to come out, and left for Kingsburg. Anxious to get outside again, they left the house by the back door and walked back to the meadow behind their house. It wasn't a particularly large piece of ground as those things go, but it was special anyway.

It was untouched since Mack bought the land, and as far as they knew, it wasn't farmed, nor had any trees been cut down in the previous unknown number of years prior to that. So it was always a treat to walk there. Especially in the early morning and late evening hours.

Even after three days of intimate contact, Lisa still took Mack's hand when they started out. He gave hers a squeeze when she did. They didn't get far before she squeezed back hard. About a hundred yards in front of them stood a large mama bear with two cubs. Even Mack was startled by the sight. Bear sightings in that part of Minnesota sometimes happened, but were rare. It was enough to stop him and make him take a step back. Slowly, they looked at each other, their eyes asking, "How is this possible?"

Mack spoke first, all be it in a whisper. "I don't think she'll bother us," he said, "as long as we don't get any closer to her. The most dangerous thing we can do is get between her and the cubs."

"I know," Lisa agreed. "Mama bears with cubs can be dangerous. But after the creatures we've had to deal with in that human trafficking bunch, she looks downright friendly. Almost like we could walk up to her and pet her."

Mack chuckle at her comments. "It's probably a good idea we don't try that. But you're right. Compared to those…" He paused a moment before he completed his thought about the human traffickers. "You know, I can't think of what to call them. If I called them people, I'd be insulting the rest of the human race. Every other living thing on the planet has more value. I can't even refer to them as a piece of shit. Even shit has value. So as for mama over there, she's so far above what they are we can't even begin to compare them. I somehow think that would be true even if she managed to attack and kill us both."

"You're right, Mack. Because if she did, it would because of something we did wrong to cause it. It would not happen because she's evil. All those traffickers were and are total evil."

They soon learned that there was no cause for concern about the bear. In a short time she grew bored with them and sauntered away, making it obvious that she didn't much care about them one way or the other. They waited until she was out of sight anyway, before they resumed their walk.

They didn't see anything more even close to as spectacular as the bear, but they still found a lot of pleasure in all they saw. It was the small herd of deer that came closest to the excitement they got from the bear sighting.

It was dark before they returned to the house. They were both tired enough by then, to appreciate the creature comforts it afforded them. They could afford a lot more house, if that was what they wanted, but they much preferred their small, three bedroom, ranch style house. It was more than large enough for their needs, and fulfilled all their wants.

They ate a light supper, consisting of tomato soup and a grilled cheese sandwiches. After supper, showers, and dressing in comfortable nightwear, they spent the rest of the evening with soft music in the background and a good book in their hands.

When they went to bed, they were so tired their thoughts were of nothing but sleep. That was especially true after all the activity they'd been involved in recently.

When Mack turned over on his side though, Lisa snuggled up against his back. Without any conscious thought, her hand drifted down from his chest to his stomach. From there, when it slipped lower, it gained Mack's attention. It took longer than expected to fall asleep that night.

That didn't matter when morning came. Mack woke up with the sun's first rays, and Lisa quickly followed him. They couldn't help but laugh when Mack kissed her good morning, and it started all over again. So it was with a great deal of satisfaction that they finally took their showers and got ready for the day.

Once they did, just before they left the house, Mack said to Lisa, "I want you to know that even after being trapped in the house with you for three days, I love you more than ever. And as far as being trapped with you like that, my fondest hope is that it happens again. I loved it, and again, I love you even more."

"I suppose, Mack, there's a lot of ways to say it, but this is the best way I know how. I love you too, Mack Thomas. More than life itself. And as far as being trapped, I hope to be trapped with you for the rest of my life and beyond."

Mack kissed her as though he meant it, then stepped back. His face was filled with a smile when he said, "I think we should leave it at that for now. Or else we might spend the rest of our lives in this house. Not that I'd actually mind that."

"Me either," she agreed. "But you're right. Anything else, and we might never get out of here."

They both laughed, then walked over to join the rest of the family for breakfast.

CHAPTER 19

Even though they called themselves mafia, the family was independent of any other organization. Their name was common in Minnesota, which is where they were from. It was Olson. They now lived in Georgia. Not because they liked Georgia so much better than Minnesota, it was more because of Minnesota's winters. Barry Olson, the patriarch of the family, hated the long, cold winters, where all too often too many activities were curtailed because everything was buried under uncountable tons of snow.

It took them many years to become wealthy enough to move the entire family from Minnesota to Georgia. The family, with Barry's work direction, started their road to wealth growing marijuana plants, processing and selling the end product. When that proved to be profitable, they graduated to any drugs they could produce themselves.

As time went on, because of their drug dealing they became acquainted with all manner of criminals and criminal enterprises. The men in the family quickly learned, from the kind of people they associated with, that women were also a valuable commodity.

They drifted into the business of selling them, on a small scale, by providing specific types of women to wealthy men as they were ordered. As that business grew, they built a network of men who did most of the kidnaping of women for them. That enabled them to grow the business of trafficking in women to the point they had markets for any and all the young, pretty girls they could acquire or grab themselves. And that made them wealthy enough to move to Georgia.

Life was good to them. Until now, that is. Now, it was another story. That bunch of do-gooders in Clayborne County had caused an immeasurable amount of trouble for them. Their entire Minnesota network was now in a shambles. Given it was the major supplier of women, it was hurting them financially. Enough so, that it was actually affecting everyone's lifestyle.

Worse than that, they were no longer able to provide an adequate supply of girls to their biggest customer, which was a mining company headquartered in Brazil. They had vast holdings throughout South America, and many of their mines were located far from normal civilization. Providing their miners with a constant stream of new, fresh women, was one of the major reasons they were able to keep people on the job.

Now, with the women in shorter supply, unrest was beginning to surface here and there in the mines. That meant the mining company executives were putting intense pressure on the Olsons to get their operation up and running to full capacity as soon as possible.

They were doing everything they could to accomplish that, but the main problem they had was the fact that most of the men from states other than Minnesota were less reliable than the Minnesotans were. Also, for a reason no one was sure of, females from the midwestern part of the United States were the miner's favorite.

After a couple of weeks, struggling to get things up and running again, Barry decided it was time to do whatever it took to get the Minnesota network back. He brought the family together to see if anyone had any ideas about how to do that.

"I'm not sure it's worth it," his oldest son, Jeff, said. "We've been trying to do something about those people for a long time now. All it's done is cost us money and personnel."

"Still, there's got to be a way," Barry argued.

"I've got some ideas," claimed the youngest son, Craig.

"Really," said the older brother. "And what might they be?" He had no confidence in his younger brother, and it showed in his voice.

"Change what we attack, what we go after. We've been going after them directly. Let's go after what they care about, which is at the same time is easier and safer for us to attack."

"Like, what the hell are you talking about? Breaking their TVs or something."

"No! I'm talking about going after their kids, pets, any animals, girl friends, and for some of them, even the car they drive. Anything close to them, that they care about. It'll discourage some of them. Others, it'll piss them off bad enough so they make mistakes when they try to get to us."

"Who the hell do you think is going to do all that?"

"Me. Let me pick my own men to go with me. About three or four of them. Then I'll go to Minnesota and get it done."

"You really think, after all the trouble they've given us, you can get the job done with only three or four men?"

"I'll get it done to the point we have them in enough confusion to allow us to finish them. When that time comes, I probably will need more help. But for now, to start, three or four is all I need."

"I don't think it'll work," Jeff said, "but if you want to try it, I'm not going to bother arguing with you about it."

"I have to differ with you," Barry said. "I think it's exactly what we need. The kid came up with a good idea this time." He looked at the youngest son. "When do you think you can get it done."

"Fairly soon. The first thing I want to do is go to Minnesota with just one of the men, to check things out. Any more of us to start and we might attract more attention than what we want to."

"That sounds like something that could take quite a while?" Jeff complained. "If it does, we might be better off to just go up there right now, and start shooting as soon as we get there."

"The problem is, we've been there and done that. The last five we sent with that useless sheriff were the best we had. Now there isn't but one of them left, and he's in jail."

"That's enough arguing," Barry told them. "We try it the kids way first. If it doesn't work out, we'll hire an army if we have to, but one way or the other, we'll get those people, and I mean all those people, the hell and gone out of our way."

The decision was made, and the oldest son wasn't happy. He hated it when any plan for any project, no matter how serious or trivial, wasn't his. He especially didn't like it when it was his youngest brother's idea. He had frequently come up with good ideas on a variety of projects and problems. Enough that Barry was beginning to question the following of tradition and turning the business over to his oldest son. The one in the middle would never be considered. He was both too lazy and too stupid. But Craig now, he was showing more promise every day.

Craig knew all that, and he loved it. Nothing in his world was more satisfying to him than showing up his older brother, Jeff. The two had a strong dislike for each other, so winning a competition between them was a special moment for either one of them when they won.

And this was a big win for the younger of them, so he started to get ready for it with a lot of enthusiasm. So much so that he never even slightly considered how much pain he would cause others to accomplish his goals.

To the surprise of everyone, including the middle brother, Tim, that's who he was taking with him to check out the possibilities in Clayborne County.

CHAPTER 20

Mack, along with almost everyone connected to the Clayborne County Sheriff's Department, was finding it a joy to go to work every morning. It wasn't like there were no problems to take care of. Life was still going on so there were still a liberal amount of accidents happening and crimes being committed. Now though, for the first time in a long time, they didn't have the burden of hired killers constantly stalking them. A problem, they hoped, they wouldn't have for a very long time, if ever again.

Lisa, more than anyone, was finding pleasure in the freedom she had riding solo as she patrolled the county each day. Like everyone, she had her tough moments. But now she could go ahead and do what needed to be done without constantly looking over her shoulder. This proved to be especially true after a bad gun accident out in the county. It was a fair distance from Kingsburg, so it took extra time for the ambulance to arrive.

Two eight year old boys were playing war with a couple of twenty-two rifles their parents gave them the previous Christmas. They'd been given safety training, and had done some small game hunting with their fathers, so they were sure they knew all they needed to know about guns.

When they first went out, they shot at all sorts of targets, be it a squirrel, sparrow, or butterfly. It didn't take long for the boredom to set in. As they walked along the top of a hillside, one of the boys moved down to the bottom of the hill.

To ease his boredom, and to have some fun, he shot the ground next to the boy at the top of the hill. That startled the kid, then he laughed. He decided to have some fun of his own, and put a bullet in a tree not far from the other boys head.

As incredibly stupid things often do, the game escalated until the boy at the top of the hill caught a bullet in his arm. He fell, bleeding profusely. As stupid as the boys were behaving. the one who did the shooting was smart enough to immediately call 911. Lisa was close, so she got there in a couple of minutes.

Without a thought about anything else, she put a tourniquet on the kids arm, then did everything she could to keep him from going into shock. After the ambulance took over and then hauled the kid to the hospital, she thought about what just happen. The fact that she was able to one hundred percent concentrate on assisting the kid made the whole ordeal go much smoother. For that she was grateful.

Later that day, when they managed a coffee break together, she told Mack about it.

"I know what you mean," he said. "It seems like a different world from the one we were living in so long. Having it stay this way is something we can only hope for. I wish there was something we could do to for sure keep it this way, but there isn't."

"Now, Mack, don't go getting all pessimistic on me. We've just got to keep it this way. Maybe we can somehow make sure we never get another organized group like those human traffickers."

"That would be great. The problem is, we can't yet be sure we've eliminated the last group."

"I don't know, but it sure seems like we did. We've killed or arrested all the locals, not to mention the hired killers."

"True, but there is probably still some, if not a lot, of that family in Georgia. I'm hoping they'll stay the hell away from us now, but it's still too early to know they will."

"I know you're right," she said, "but I'm going to make the best of what it is now anyway."

"Good," Mack agreed. "That's what you should do."

"Yes, me and everyone else. Older people say this all the time, and I have to agree with them. Life is short, so make use of every moment. After all that you and I have been through, we, more than anyone, should take that advice."

"I agree. I also think that to a large extent that's what we do. And the good thing is, so does my family."

Mack was right with that assessment of them. And that's what Theresa Thomas, his father Ben's wife, was doing. She managed the community garden Mack started. It was a volunteer job. A job she did because she loved working with people in the garden. She often stopped to answer questions from people who had plots growing there. She was talking to a woman about the various reasons the leaves on her tomato plants were turning brown, when a big man, driving a beat up, Chevy pickup and wearing an equally beat up pair of coveralls drove into the parking lot.

He stormed out of the truck, walked up to a woman on her hands and knees, meticulously weeding her plot, and kicked her hard on her backside. The woman fell on her face, but didn't utter a sound. It was immediately obvious that she was used to rough treatment.

"Now get the hell up, bitch, and get your ass back home," the man yelled. "This is the last time I'm ever going to tell you to stay home and away from this place. It's evil and against God's will to do what they do here. Eve was thrown out of the garden for a reason. Next time I catch you here, when I get done with you, you won't be able to come here or go anywhere again. I know what you do here is just whore around."

Theresa, being who she was, couldn't sit back and let the man do what he was doing. She confronted him. Looking him in the eye, she asked, "What the hell do you think you're doing?"

"Ain't none a yer concern, you whore among whores" he spit back. "Now get the hell out a my way so I can get this bitch on her way home where she damn well belongs."

"No," Theresa answered, her voice sharp, "you'll do no such thing. We don't allow your kind of behavior in this garden. It'll be best if you leave now."

"Screw you," he said, grabbing the woman by her hair to pull her to her feet.

Theresa was holding her cell phone, so she snapped a picture of him. He tried to take the phone away from her, but she kept it out of his hands. Frustrated, he hit her. It was a sound blow to the side of her face. She went down. As soon as she hit the ground, she speed dialed Mack.

Knowing she wouldn't call him without good reason, he answered, "Is something wrong?"

"I just got hit by a man trying to abuse a woman here in the garden. I think I could use some help."

Mack and Lisa were just leaving Katy's Kafe when the call came, so they both went to the garden. It twas only a few blocks away, so they were there as Theresa was getting to her feet.

The big man was kicking the abused woman when they got to the garden. Lisa, being who she was, instantly attacked the man. She moved in close, a used both fists to pummel his protruding his stomach. He doubled over before he could respond any other way. As his head dropped low enough, she clasped her hands together and slammed them down on the back of his neck. She kneed his face on his way to the ground.

It all happened so fast that he was face down on the ground before Mack could pull her back away from him. She was shaking with anger when he did.

"Do you think maybe that you might have over done it some?" he asked, but kept his voice soft.

She turned her head to face him. As their eyes met, she said, "After what he was doing to her, you still ask me that! Is it now okay for men to beat on women, but not for women to defend themselves?"

"I didn't mean it that way, Lisa. I just wondered if you really needed to knee his face on his way down."

"Damn right I did. And if I wouldn't have been in control of my temper, I'd have kicked his teeth out when he was on the ground."

Theresa interrupted. "Lisa's right, Mack. He deserved everything he got. I have a video of what he did to her," she pointed to the abused woman, "on my camera. He also assaulted me. I will be pressing charges against him, regardless of what she or anyone else does."

"I sure can't blame you for that," Mack said. He turned to Lisa. "And I'm sorry I said what I said to you in the wrong way. I mostly meant to give you a back-handed compliment on the way you took him out. I've got no more time for men like him than what you do."

"I know that. I'm sorry too, Mack, for getting so upset with you, when I know better."

The abusive bully of a man was just now rising from the short slumber Lisa gave him. When he was on his feet, he shook himself, trying to bring himself back to full reality. He turned to the abused woman, who was still on the ground, now curled into a fetal position. Without hesitation, he kicked her again, this time in the small of her back. She groaned softly.

"Get up, you whore bitch," he screamed. "You've defiled yourself in God's eyes enough for one day." He kicked her again.

Lisa held back, wanting Mack to respond this time. He did. He pulled the man by the arm until they were facing each other.

Mack didn't hit the man. Instead he said, "I want you to know. There is no God here on earth, in heaven, or even in hell, who wants you to be beating on women in general, or any woman in particular. The so-called God you're talking about is normally called the devil. And the only one around here who has defiled anything is you."

"She's my wife, so it's my duty as her husband to keep her from sin. God doesn't tolerate the kind of behavior of the people here."

"Really? Gardening, growing food that is healthy and safe is doing something wrong? How did you ever manage to cram that much stupidity into that tiny little brain of yours."

"I'm not stupid. No where in the bible is there anything about eating tomatoes or peppers. When Jesus fed the masses it was bread and wine. We aren't meant to eat most stuff people do now. So being here, in this garden, is a mortal sin. I'm trying to save her soul."

Everyone who had been working in their garden plots was now gathered around them. They were, each and every one of them, shaking their heads yes when Mack spoke. When the big bully said something, the head shakes were negative.

Regardless of what those around him might have thought, Mack answered him with his own truth. "All you're doing is throwing your weight around. You think you're being a big, macho male, beating on someone who can't defend herself against you. Well, macho man, a few minutes ago, you got your ass kicked by a woman less than half your size. And the truth is, if she wasn't the decent person she is, she'd do it again. Only worse this time."

"She cheated. She caught me by surprise. Ain't no other way she could do it again."

"You sure about that? Maybe I should let her do to you what she'd like to do to you. You ready for that?"

"No. If I beat her, you'd put me in jail for doing it. So let's stop this now. All I want to do is take my wife home where she'll be safe from sins of you who simply don't know the true God."

"Well," Mack explained, "one thing's sure. That's not going to happen. You will be going to jail. To start with, you'll be charged with the assault of Theresa here. Second, we have videos of you abusing your wife. You might get away with that at home, but this time you did it in public. So we can hang you for it even if your wife doesn't press charges."

"All I did was hit her," he pointed at Theresa, "one time. It wasn't even that hard either. As for my wife, it's not only my right as her husband to insure that she behave, it's my sworn duty to do so."

A total disgust with the man flowed through Mack after his last comment. "Sworn duty? To who?"

"To God, of course. I have sworn to God to uphold his law the best ways I can. If that means I'm forced to discipline my sinful wife, a wife who thinks she should be allowed to make decisions on her own, then so be it."

"You are full of shit," Mack said. "I just wish that people who think… no, you don't think. You're not equipped to think. I wish people who believe the bullshit you do, could get smart enough just long enough, to know just how stupid you sound."

"Are you now saying that you think my faith in God is stupid?"

"Pretty much, yes. That's exactly what I think. About you, about your faith, and about the macho image you think you have. Mostly you are, in my opinion, a stupid, useless, bully boy, who uses a nonexistent God as an excuse for an endless amount of bad behavior."

"You are going to go to hell for saying that," the man said.

Mack laughed. He'd listened enough and so had heard enough. It had been all too frequent in his life that he'd heard the God told me so argument for what was bad behavior. It was used by anyone from serial killers to the president of the United States.

He cuffed the man, took him in and locked him up. Lisa brought the wife with her when she and Theresa joined Mack for completion of the paperwork.

The only thing Dale said when they told him the story was, "Lock him up."

The wife was afraid to press charges against the husband, so Lisa did the only thing she could do. She brought the woman home. The woman thanked Lisa for the help after she was dropped off. Lisa only nodded her head in return. She knew that the lady would be beaten again. Probably a lot more, for the rest of her life, as long and she and her husband were both alive. Or until he killed her with one of his beatings.

On the way home, Lisa thought about the conversation Mack had with the man. She disagreed with what the man said about God, and agreed with what Mack said. But in spite of that, she disagreed on one thing. No matter what else, she couldn't shake the idea that somehow, somewhere, there needed to be some kind of spirit or God or something way above what mere humans were. Because if there wasn't, what could be the purpose of any of it?

She knew though, what Mack would say to that. "The purpose to all of it is life itself. And that's why we should always have respect for it. In all its forms. Not just the human ones. And the real truth of it all, if you look closely to the whole planet earth, the only living creature on it who often doesn't seem to fit in with the rest of life, it's us two legged beasts. God or no God."

CHAPTER 21

Craig Olson led his somewhat older brother, Tim, up the stairs to the plane. Tim, the middle son of Bradly Olson, wasn't completely sure what he was doing there. He appreciated that his younger brother was giving him a chance to prove himself, he just wasn't sure yet what he'd have to do to accomplish it. All he knew was the fact that there would eventually be a lot of killing involved.

Not that he minded killing. It was actually, something he rather enjoyed. He had, now and then, picked out one of the girls they purchased for his own use. Always, it seemed, there was nothing left to do when he finished, but put them out of their misery. And doing that, in the end, was what gave him the most joy.

Even though he didn't understand much about the family business, or what they were trying to accomplish on this trip, he was very much looking forward to it. The idea of the killing alone was enough to excite him.

Also along for the ride were two well paid professionals. They were along for the sole purpose of easing the boredom of the plane ride. They were so good at what they did, that they actually did fill most of the brother Tim's time. It was an easy task for them, given his short staying power. Normally, they were often used by the family to entertain special guests, an often more difficult job. People like the mine owners that they did so much business with could be extremely demanding. Because they could consistently fulfill those demands, it made them too valuable for anyone to do anything to damage them.

This fact upset Tim, so it didn't matter how good the treatment on the flight was, he was disappointed and whiny when he got off the plane. He complained to his brother on the ride from the plane to the hotel. Craig finally got so tired of it that as soon as they settled in, he made some calls. Soon, he brought a woman to Tim's room.

In a low voice he said to his brother, "when you finish, you must do it quietly."

Before the night was over, they managed to open an empty room on a different floor, and dump the body of the lady on the bed there. Because it wasn't occupied and didn't need cleaning, it wasn't discovered until after the brothers checked out of the hotel. Because the woman was a known prostitute, the police didn't put forth full effort to catch whoever committed the murder.

Their first full day in Minnesota, the brothers drove north. They stopped for lunch at Katy's Kafe in Kingsburg. Looking around at the number of sheriff's deputies and local police eating there, Craig put it on the list of places to attack. Especially during the noon meal.

After lunch, the drove up to Jackstone County. They stayed in a local motel there, owned by a man who was once a friend of the former sheriff, Tod Mcintire. They knew it was about the safest place there was in the area.

Time was valuable to them, with so many things and people to check out, so they didn't spend much time at the motel. From the first full day, they started their day early, and often worked into the night.

As they moved from place to place, Craig found a lot of people, places, and things he was sure would be ideal to destroy. He wanted to cause as much severe damage as possible. At the same time, once the hoped for holocaust started, he wanted to mix up the devastation as much as possible. He planned to kill two or three people to start. He would leave the dangerous ones alone, and go after wives, friends and children of the dangerous ones. Second, fires would be started. Homes, garages, cars, and a local business or two. Finally, animals. Any and all pets. He especially found the horses on the Thomas ranch interesting. So much so, that he considered killing some or all of them first.

Tim was different. His choices were simpler. People? Simple, kill them all. Homes and businesses. Again simple. Burn each and every one of them. Animals. A total slaughter was the best answer.

Cruising around, making notes as they checked out the people, places, and things, it went smoothly. Much better than expected. But Tim quickly became somewhat of a problem.

He constantly complained about something. From the time they left the plane, he bitched about the weather. Minnesota was in the middle of one of its typical summer cold spells.

"You know," he complained to Craig, "it never gets this cold in Georgia. You should of told me how cold it is here. I woulda stayed home. I don't need this kind of shit."

"I couldn't tell you something I didn't know."

"You shoulda checked the weather channel. They woulda told you it was like this here."

"I did. I checked a lot of channels. They all said the same thing. Sunny and mild."

"All of them was wrong then. I sure don't like it. I plain don't like being here. Wouldn't even if it wasn't so damn cold."

"What else don't you like?"

"Being bored. Back home, there's always plenty to do. Here, all we do is ride around and look at stuff. If we're gonna do that all the time, then we should kill someone. Or maybe burn something down. What would be even more fun is to go after them horses we looked at. I don't like them damn things. They stink. They always smell like horses. Before we go home, I want to kill me a couple of them."

"I'll have to think about that," Craig told him. "We're here on a reconnaissance mission, to get the information we need so we can destroy these people when we return."

"I know that, but even if we kill a few horses before we go back, they won't know what we got planned for them."

"You'll have to wait and see. And no matter what, we don't do anything like that until just before we get on the plane to go home."

"Well, okay, Craig, I can wait on them horses. But I sure do have a need for a woman. You think maybe I could get me one?"

"I don't know. After what you did to the last one, those that have some won't let you use them. They're in short supply around here now anyway. That damn sheriff and his deputies in that Clayborne County are the ones who caused them to be hard to find. But that's why we're here. To get the info we need to come back here and set things straight."

"I know, but there should be a woman out there for me anyway."

"Well there isn't, so just forget about it for now."

Tim looked at his brother, sneered, and thought, "Like hell there ain't no woman for me. There's a bunch I been watching. And they all ride that bus what loads them up and hauls them home after school everyday. There's a real cute one I want. I'm gonna figure out a way to go after her. She's gonna be tot's of fun."

CHAPTER 22

The first time Mack saw the two men driving through town, he paid them little attention. The third time, he took notice. He checked out the vehicle they were in and as he suspected, it was a rental. The name on the rental agreement proved to be fictitious. That was all it took to raise his suspicions of the men to a high level.

He talked to Dale about them, and he agreed that the men needed watching. The department was then informed that the men should be watched.

Having the entire department intermittently watching the men proved beneficial. Watching them that way never raised the two men's suspicions. That failure on their part also allowed the department to get a closer look at what they were doing. It didn't take long then, for everyone to be sure they were up to no good.

Mack and Dale would like to have arrested them, but since they'd broken no laws they couldn't do it. They did, however, continue their surveillance of the men.

They finally got a break on the afternoon of the third day of the men's visit. Tim was let loose by his brother, and was out and about, wandering the streets of Kingsburg. He stopped first at the grade school, to watch the kids outside at recess. He especially like watching the girls. From his viewpoint, most of them were old enough to satisfy him. After all, they were females. What other purpose could they possibly have that mattered as much as satisfying him.

The deputy who watched him as he stood there, found him to be as disgusting as anything she'd ever seen. Especially the way he rubbed himself as he watched. She called his activity in, and was instructed to keep an eye on him as long as she could without raising his suspicions.

Five minutes later he noticed her. She gave him what she hoped he'd take as a friendly wave, and drove away. They lost track of him for a while then. He was next spotted about a block from the middle school, walking away. A short time later he rejoined his brother.

"Feel better now?" Craig asked him.

"It was okay. I only seen one of them deputies. She was parked for a time, when I was watching the kid's playing outside at the grade school."

"What the hell was you doin' there?"

"Nothin'. Just watching them. I didn't hurt nobody."

"Maybe not, but there ain't much better ways to get a cop wondering about you, than what hanging around kids will. So please try to be smart for once in your life, and stay the hell away from the kids."

"Are you sayin' I ain't smart?"

"We both know you got a long way to go in that department. I didn't bring you along because I thought you were at all smart. I brought you along so's we could prove to the old man that you and me are every bit as good as that damn brother of ours."

"Are you sayin' you don't like him?"

"Do you?"

"Not really. But ain't we supposed to?"

"Maybe. I guess I might if he wasn't so damn chicken shit all the time. It seems like he ain't never said one good thing about no idea I ever had. Always pushing the old man to do it different than what I say."

"You mean you had me come with you this time to show him I could do something right?"

"Yeah, that and I just wanted you along."

"Be damned. I always thought you didn't like me much."

"Sometimes I don't. But you're the best brother I got. So here you are."

"You're my best too," Tim said, but thought, "Best or not, I'm not goin' to be doin' everything you want. You're just like the rest of them, always telling me what to do. Not this time. This time I'm gonna get what I want. And doin' the one I want is goin' to be special. I ain't never done one that young before."

The next day, Tim asked Craig to let him spend the afternoon at the motel. He stayed inside until it was time for school to let out. He waited for a certain young girl to leave that small town's version of a combination grade and middle school. He had seen her the previous morning as she walked to school. Her route took her close enough to the motel to make it easy for hime to notice.

This day, he followed her home. She lived in a small, story and a half house that was built in the early fifties. It was in decent shape, but had some minor problems that the average home owner would have repaired. The lawn also needed some work, so Tim strongly suspected that the girls lived with a single mother. If not, and there were two parents, it was likely the father wasn't worth much, and wouldn't be any kind of a problem for Tim. He was big and strong enough to be willing to take on most men if he was forced to.

He watched long enough to be sure the girl was in the house alone. He approached it from the back. When he checked it, it was only locked at the doorknob itself. There was no deadbolt. He opened it easily with a credit card and went in.

He found the girl, Dawn Swanson, in the kitchen, heating a can of soup on the stove. He was almost as quiet as he wanted to be as he crept up behind her. He was close enough to grab her when she first saw him and tried to scream. He slapped his hand around her mouth before she could scream enough for anyone to hear her.

Dawn was a pretty girl, with long dark hair. She was only thirteen, and still going through puberty, so her body hadn't yet filled out completely. Nor had it finished growing.

She tried to fight him, but didn't have any kind of chance of stopping him from anything he wanted to do. She was just too small. Even if she'd been full grown, there would have been little she could do to fight him off. Her only chance would have been some intensive self defense training. Something she didn't have.

In spite of her constant struggles, he managed to pick her up and carry her to a bedroom. He dropped her on the bed, his hand still over her mouth, ripped off her clothes, and raped her. Painful as it was for her, this first time wasn't as bad for her as it could have been. He only lasted a little over a minute.

Rather than be embarrassed by his lack of control, he smiled. "That's the way I like it the first time," he said. "Quick, so now you know what I can do."

Dawn closed her eyes and kept them closed the whole time. She continued to keep them closed as he bragged to her about how great he was. She cried the whole time. He slapped her when he noticed her tears.

"Don't be crying you little bitch," he said. "What I'm giving you now is something you won't never get nowhere else as good."

Getting what he was giving her was something she prayed she'd never get anywhere. She tried to curl herself into a ball, trying to hide her naked body, as he sat there staring at her. He reacted with a vicious slap across her face when she did, only for doing it.

It didn't take long then, for the bruises to start appearing on her face, as he slapped or hit her for the slightest move he didn't like. When he raped her a second time, he was sure he'd done much better. His performance was so good, he was sure, that it would take any woman happy and satisfied. He lasted all of three to four minutes.

She was still crying and her tears aggravated him. So much, that he hit her hard a couple of times. Too hard. It surprised him when she stopped breathing after his blows. She was dead.

Killing her wasn't part of his plan. Not this soon anyway. His plan was to use her several times before he did anything else to her. Now, here he was with a dead body, and he was still less than totally satisfied. He knew he could use her body at least one more time, if he didn't wait too long. He'd done it with other women he'd killed, but even that would leave him somewhat less than fully satisfied.

It would be better than nothing though, so after some time looking at her, he used his hand to get himself ready, and did it to her again. He got a surprise though. Just as he finished, her mother came home. He heard her voice as she talked on her cell phone.

He quickly left the bed, pulled up his pants, and waited behind the bedroom door for her to come in the room. He knew she'd be concerned when she saw her daughter laying naked and so still on the bed.

He was right. The mother, Sally Swanson, soon came into the room, turning on the light with the wall switch as she did. She gasped when she saw her daughter on the bed, but Tim hit her on the back of the head as hard as he could with the butt of his gun before she could do anything. He wasn't sure if she was dead or not, but assumed she was. He stripped her slowly, salivating as her body appeared for him. He grinned and sighed with satisfaction as he raped her, not caring at all if there was any life left in her body.

When he finished with her, and rose to his feet, all his activity suddenly made him pretty much confused about what to do next. He'd always had help in the past when he needed to get rid of the body of a woman. Now he was here alone with two bodies. In his confused state, he was finding it almost impossible to figure out what to do, much less how to do it.

With his continued confusion, he roamed around the bedroom with the same confidence of a puppy experiencing its first time away from its mother. Somewhere during the third circuit of the room, the Sally woke up. She was still holding her cell phone, and almost as if it was instinct working, she took several pictures of him.

That was all she managed to do. The blow to her head still had control over her, and she lost consciousness again. He hadn't noticed that she'd been awake for a few minutes. The only thing he managed to see with her was her near perfect figure. He loved the fact he could see all oft it.

Even so, he worried himself into a frenzied state about what to do. He then decided to see if using the bodies again would help clear his head. He did Dawn first, and unlike the other two times, he managed to last almost ten minutes. He was proud of himself as he pulled away from her. It never occurred to him why he lasted so much longer. He didn't notice the temperature of the body. It was much colder.

It was different with Sally. She was warm, and even though there wasn't much left of him, his time with her was very short. It didn't occur to him that she was still warm, and therefore alive. He was sure she was dead, therefore she must be dead.

For another ten minutes or so he paced the floor, but he didn't come to any conclusion about what to do. He only became ever more agitated. The only rational thought he had was knowing he needed to do something soon. The longer he waited, the more chance there was that he might be caught there.

Finally, when he couldn't come up with any idea about what to do, he did the only thing he could do. He walked away, leaving the back door of the house open. He was lucky, and walked back to the motel room without anyone noticing. There, he waited quietly for his brother to return, all the time trying to decide whether to tell Craig what he did. In the end, he decided not to. He was sure by then that he was safe. At least for a while. So it made little sense to tell Craig and get yelled at for what he did.

What never occurred to him was the fact that Sally was actually still alive. And worse for him than that, the fact that she took several pictures of him.

It was those pictures that the mother was dealing with now. She'd already checked her daughter and knew without a doubt that Dawn was dead. But even though she was heart broken, she knew she had to put them somewhere that they'd be safe. She knew that leaving them in the phone without backing them up would be a mistake.

She'd lived her whole life in Jackstone County, and had watched it go from a typical rural community where people looked out for each other, to a place you never trusted your neighbor or the local police. So she downloaded her cell phone onto her computer. From there, she copied the photos to a modern storage device, and then found a still new writable CD to put the pictures on. She labeled the plastic case she put the CD in, 'Taxes' and put it in a file with other financial documents.

She then first called the state police, waited a few minutes, and called the sheriff. She didn't bother to call the local Baptism Towers police or 911. To start with, the police were useless, and second, corrupt. If she would have called 911, they would have been the first there. She hoped then, that the state police would be the first to arrive. She just couldn't be sure the sheriff could be trusted. Not after all the things the ex-sheriff who'd been recently arrested was involved in.

She got lucky, and the first to arrive was a state patrolman. She'd somehow held herself together until then, but as soon as he approached him she broke down. The reason he was there suddenly swept over her.

When the feelings one always gets, with a loss the magnitude of losing a daughter were realized, her emotions took total control.

The young man from the state police was trained for situations like this and called for backup. He then did everything he could to calm her. The acting sheriff, however, reacted differently. As soon as he examined the scene, he decided to cover for whoever was responsible. He was fairly certain, the person responsible was very likely involved with what was left of the human trafficking organization. Since he knew they'd need everyone with any kind of experience to get it up and running again, that person needed protecting.

So he lied about what the evidence told him, and accused Sally of the murder. He claimed that she caught Dawn having sex with her boyfriend, and that she got so angry about it that she killed Dawn because of it. As far as the fictitious boyfriend went, he got lucky and escaped.

Lucky for Sally, the state police backup team arrived, and took over the crime scene. They also took charge of her, and didn't allow the acting sheriff to question or otherwise intimidate her.

They also took charge of her camera, and downloaded the pictures and the entire contents of the phone onto their computer system. That gave Sally hope that they might catch whoever it was that killed Dawn, but still left some serious doubts about the outcome. There had been too many times in the past that rapes and murders of women and girls in and around Jackstone County hadn't been solved. This time, she hoped for a different ending.

CHAPTER 23

When Mack met Dale for coffee that morning, Lisa and Paul joined them. Dale had asked them too. As soon as they all had their coffee in front of them, Dale opened a folder and gave each of them a sheet of paper from it.

"Yesterday a thirteen year old girl was murdered in her own home, up in Jackstone County. Her mother discovered the murderer in the bedroom with the girl when she came home from work. In spite of a severe blow to her head, which knocked her out, she managed to take several photos of the man. They're on the sheet I just gave you."

It didn't take Mack more than a glance at the photos to recognize the man pictured. "He's one of the two men we've been watching," he said. "He's usually with the other guy. I've wondered about them. They never broke any laws that we know of. From what I could tell, it mostly seemed like they were checking out various things or places in town."

"I only saw them once," Lisa said. "They were close to home. They were driving slow, and it seemed like they were watching the pasture we keep the horses in."

"I've watched them a couple of times too," Paul added. "Unfortunately, I didn't catch them doing anything illegal."

"Do you have any more info on him?" Mack asked.

"Not a whole lot." Dale answered. "Only that his DNA is a close match to a Barry Olson. He at one time was arrested and tried for rape, so his DNA is on record. He got off on a technicality. From the reports I read on the crime, there was a strong suspicion that the judge for the trial was bribed."

"Where is this Barry Olson now?"

"He and his family live near Gainesville, Georgia."

"Any chance the killer will be arrested in Georgia?"

"Not without more proof. What will give us that proof is his DNA. The goal now is to catch him and get it. If we can do that, we won't need to worry about Georgia."

"Maybe not concerning this crime. But those two guys are here for some reason. The question is, will that reason go away just because we manage to arrest the one who committed the murder, or is there something else going on. And if so, what?"

"I wonder the same thing," Lisa said. "Given the way things seem to go, this gives me the feeling that those guys are here for a lot more than to rape and murder a thirteen year old girl."

"I have to agree with Lisa and Mack," Paul said. "So more than just look for the guy who committed the murder, we have to keep our eyes open to almost anything."

Dale gave them a grim smile. "That's exactly why I wanted all three of you here this morning. I'm about as sure as I could be that something real damn serous is going on. I'm also sure that we'd better do all we can to get ready for it. No matter what *it* is."

When the break was done and the three of them resumed their patrols of the county, the thoughts about something serious going on wouldn't stop running through Mack's head. He had no doubts now that something was going on. His only question was how serious was it?

It was the same question Craig Olson was asking. How serious was it going to be? But even though the question was the same, the subject matter was different. His concern was over his brother Tim's latest incredibly stupid mistake.

"Why did you have to do something so stupid?" he asked Tim. "Going after that girl. Raping that girl. Killing that girl. Those were things you did that were so stupid that I find them unbelievable. There was absolutely no excuse for doing them. But you couldn't leave it with that. You had to follow through with a couple of things so stupid that they are incomprehensible."

"I don't know what you mean," Tim whined in return. "I just hit her. She wasn't supposed to die."

"I wasn't talking about the girl when I said what you did is impossible to comprehend. I was talking about letting the mother take pictures of you. And if that wasn't enough, you left her alive. How could you be so stupid?"

"I didn't know she took my picture. If I would of knowed what she done, I would have not let her."

"Maybe, but you left her alive. Even you are smart enough to know that when you do something as bad as kill people, you don't leave anyone behind who is still alive."

"I thought she was dead. The last time I done her, she sure seemed dead. She didn't move at all."

"That's how you decided? She didn't move when you raped her?"

"Well, yeah. What else was I supposed to do?"

"Damnit, Tim, that's being extremely stupid, even for you. Did you listen to her heart? You can hear it beat when people are alive."

"Well, I didn't know what to do, so I forgot to check her heart. I don't think I know how anyway."

"Probably not. You are stupid beyond stupid. And because of how stupid you are, we're going to have to go back to Georgia tomorrow. And we've only completed about half of what I wanted to get done on this mission."

"I don't think I'm so stupid. I'm just not so smart as you. And I don't want to go home tomorrow. You promised me I could kill them horses. Are you going take me to kill them tonight? I really want to kill them tonight."

"No. We aren't going anywhere until it's time to leave for the plane tomorrow."

"But I want to kill them horses. Them people shouldn't get to have them. They like them too much. Besides, they play like they are sheriffs. But they don't ride their horses when they're being sheriffs. If they were real sheriffs, they would ride their horses, instead of driving around in pickup trucks."

"When we come back to get rid of all these people around here, you can kill horses then."

"I think we should kill them now. It will really scare them. That Mack and that Lisa, they don't get scared so easy. But they really like them horses, so if we kill them now, they probably might be real scared when we come back from Georgia."

"It will take more than killing horses to scare any of the people in that sheriff's office. So we're not going to do anything but wait for the plane. If I could have gotten it here right away, we'd be on it now."

"Then let me go alone to kill them. I bet I can kill all of them without no help at all."

"I think it's time for you to shut the hell up about the horses. There's simply no need to kill them now."

"Maybe not, Craig. Not for you anyway. But there is for me. I really do need to kill them. I don't feel so good when I go to places like this where everybody and everything is bad to us, and not kill something. Killing them horses would be a good thing to do. Even better, it would feel really good."

"That's what all of this is about for you, isn't it, Tim? You feeling good. You haven't been much real help since we got here. Now you've screwed things up by killing that girl, leaving her mother alive, and letting her take your picture. But even all that wasn't enough. Now you want to kill some horses because it might make you feel good. Get real. We've got more important things to do than make you feel good."

Tim gave up trying to convince Craig that he should get the chance to kill the horses that Mack, Lisa, and the rest of those Thomases owned. There was just no way he was going to convince Craig to let him. But he decided to see if he could find a way to do it without his help. No matter what, he knew that killing them would hurt and scare all of that family. Losing their horses had to scare them. Even more, it had to hurt them. He knew it would because if they were his horses, it would hurt and scare him if someone killed them. But best of all, there was nothing that felt so good, that gave him such a sense of power, as killing did. And killing something as big as a horse, he was sure, would enhance that sense of power.

But at that moment, Mack was having thoughts of killing too. His, however, were anything but being about the joy to be found in killing.

They were, in fact, just the opposite. Mack instead found the constant killing horrifying. It was something he wanted to be able to wish away. Something he knew would never be possible.

So he tried, instead, to concentrate on what they could all do to prevent further killing. Something, he was sure now, that if they didn't find a way to stop, there would be more of. He was also sure that whatever trouble was coming, it would also include other acts of terrorism. The problem at the moment was that it never occurred to him that anyone would go after their horses.

CHAPTER 24

It was near midnight, and Mack gave up on trying to sleep. He tried to leave the bed quietly, but Lisa woke up anyway. She reached up and touched his arm before he got off the bed.

"What is it, Mack? What's wrong?" she asked.

"Nothing I can easily explain. I just can't get the idea out of my head, that this time the people who want to get revenge agains us, who want us dead, are going to try anything and everything they can to accomplish it."

"This has happened before, too many times, but it didn't keep you awake. You usually can sleep, when you're tired, no matter what the problem."

"I know," Mack said, "but this time…" before he could finish, there was a loud knock on their front door. Mack slipped his pants on and went to answer it. It was Roy and Wanda.

"I'm sorry, Mack," she said as she struggled to bring her gasping breath back to normal. "But I have to know, did you have the dream too?"

"I've been awake all night. Something wouldn't let me sleep. The feeling that something god-awful is going to happen wouldn't let me. What was your dream about?"

"Something *god-awful* happening. A loud scream first. It wasn't human. It sounded like a bad hurt horse. Then two more screams. First an angry horse, then a human screamed in terror. When I ran to it there was blood on the ground. Lots of blood, Then someone moaned, and I woke up.

Mack stared at her, then remembered Lisa's comments at the coffee break that morning about the two men looking at the horses. Before he could say anything, Lisa joined them.

"I heard what you told Mack," she said. "Are you having those dreams again?"

Roy answered for her. "It sure looks like it, Lisa. But so far as I know, this is the first time she's had one that Mack didn't have too."

"It is different," Mack agreed. "But not so much as it seems. Given the way I feel, what I've been worrying over, I don't doubt that if I would have been asleep when Wanda had the dream, I would have had it too."

"Well, now that the two of you are back in the business of seeing the future, are you seeing it well enough to do something about it?"

"I'm not sure, Roy," Wanda told him. "Not enough to do something to stop it from happening. But I am sure enough to know that we all have to be very careful now. Whatever the hell it is that's going to happen, it will sooner or later affect all of us. And I mean *all* of us. Ben, Theresa, and even Sue. Whatever it is that someone's got planned, whatever they do, they'll be coming for all of us first.'

"I've got the same feeling," Mack agreed. "I don't think we finished things up there in Jackstone county. I think we just started them."

"I've been getting the same feelings as Mack," Lisa said. "And I don't think we'll be able to stop the trouble just by arresting who ever it is that is behind all that's happening. This time, if we're going to survive what's coming, we'll need to do more."

"The question is," Roy asked, "how much farther?"

"I hate saying this," Mack answered. "I really do. But we'll have to take it as far as we have to take it."

"Meaning what?"

"Kill them all. Whoever and wherever they are."

Roy shook his head and sighed heavily at Mack's answer. Lisa and Wanda nodded their heads.

As they paused in their conversation after Mack's revelation, their silence leaving the impression that they were waiting for some kind of verification of Mack's words, someone out in the horse pasture was about to give it to them.

Tim Olson had parked the car he and Craig had been using on the road, and was now approaching the horses. As he grew close to them, all but one of them shied away. The horse, Lancer, was Lisa's. She'd owned him since she was still a kid, and he was fully mature went she got him, so he was a relatively old horse now.

He was set in his ways, but in most cases his ways were good ones. The treatment he'd received, both from Lisa and his previous owners his entire life, was excellent. It had made him an exceptionally friendly animal who'd lost the normal mistrust of strangers, so he waited for Tim to come and pet his neck.

At the same time, Mack's horse, Dare, who by his born nature still had a strong distrust of strangers, moved up behind Tim. He wasn't able to understand what the problem was with Tim, but he definitely did sense that there was a problem.

As soon as Tim reached Lancer, the problem became apparent. The horse screamed in terror as the knife in Tim's hand slashed across Lancer's throat, leaving a killing wound. A second scream instantly followed the first. I was a different scream though. This one was a scream of fury as Dare rose up on his hind legs as high as a horse could reach.

A third scream followed. A human scream of pain as two hooves came crashing down on Tim's shoulders, shattering them. It was followed by three more double hoof blows on the chest of the now downed Tim.

An almost unbelieving group of four people rushed into the pasture then. Dare bobbed his head as a greeting to Mack, then backed away from the now seriously battered Tim.

Lisa ignored Tim, knelt next to Lancer, and held his head in her lap. Silent tears ran heavily down her cheeks as she did her best to say goodbye to a friend as dear as anyone could ever ask for.

Roy was seething in anger, every bone in his body wanting to kick Tim's face in. Wanda had her cell phone, and started to call 911. Mack stopped her.

"Not yet," he said, "the horse is already dead."

"What about him?" she pointed to Tim.

"Not until we have a little discussion."

"But he could die."

Mack shrugged and knelt down so he could hear answers tp the questions he wanted to ask.

"What in the hell did you think you were doing, coming here and killing horses?"

Tim coughed as he struggled to answer. "I came here to show you some of what's coming."

"Really? You plan on killing some dogs next?"

"Yeah," Tim choked out. "and some kids too."

"Like that little girl you raped and murdered."

His breathing grew heavier, falling into heavy gasps. He looked at Mack, trying to show him a mean expression. He failed at it as the pain he was in showed through. He took a deep breath and said, "Much more than that. This time, ain't nothing gonna stop us. You are all gonna get dead. There ain't gonna be nothin' left. What we don't kill, we'll burn"

"Who's going to do all that?"

"We are." he gasped for breath again. "You're gonna lose this…" One more gasp and he was dead.

Mack got up slowly, then looked down on Tim one more time before telling Wanda, "You can call 911 now."

"Are you sure you want me to? You know the law. Someone will be wanting to put down Dare now."

"Anyone tries, and they won't much like me after I finish with them. All he did was try to help his friend and defend himself."

Lisa was now on her feet and standing next to them. "Mack's right," she said. "No one is going to get anywhere near Dare. They try, and I'll be forced to put a bullet in them."

"I've got a better idea," Mack explained. "Roy, will you go get a bucket of warm, soapy water. We'll wash the hooves of all the horses. Then let them try to figure out which horse to go after."

With Wanda's help, they completed the task long before anyone from the support team thought to ask about the horses. The only answer they got from Mack, Roy, or Wanda was, "I have no idea which horse did it."

Lisa's answer was, "I don't know, but if I did I'd breed it if I could. The world needs more horses like that. Horses that can improve life for everything and everyone the way this one did."

Dale arrived a few minutes later. One of the support team people approached him as soon as he got out of his car. He handed Dale a sheet of paper and showed him a driver's license and a motel card key. He looked at them, then found Mack.

"The guy on the ground is one Tim Olson, from Gainesville, Georgia," he said, "and he was staying at the motel in Baptism Towers, up in Jackstone County."

"Then that's where we're going now, right?" Mack asked.

"I'll be going with the State Police, Mack." Dale told him, "You and Lisa can't come along, because you'll be needed here to answer questions about what went down."

"That's just so much more technical bullshit," Mack answered. "But we'll stay here. We've got plenty to do here anyway. Burying Lisa's horse is one of them."

"Speaking of horses," Dale said, "do you know which one killed the guy?"

"Of course not," Mack told him. He knew that if he told Dale, he would be obligated to tell the animal control people which horse it was that did do the killing. That would make it far more difficult for them to keep Dare out of the hands of the control people.

"I suppose you don't," Dale agreed, understanding Mack's reason for not telling him. Like most people who have had a lot of contact with many kinds of animals, he knew that in a case like this, the horse who killed the man was infinitely more valuable than the human creature it killed. So he intentionally dropped the subject.

Dale left a short time later with several members of the state police. They were on their way to Baptism Falls, to check out the motel there. They made it a quick ride, running the whole time with lights and sirens. When they arrived, they didn't bother with any formalities. They just kicked in the motel room door.

A soundly sleeping Craig Olson meekly surrendered when he woke up with several men surrounding his bed, all pointing powerful handguns at him.

He was allowed to dress, then cuffed, loaded into a squad car, and hauled to Kingsburg, where he was locked in a cell in the sheriff's office. The state patrol had finally learned that it was a mistake to trust any law enforcement group from Jackstone County. Dale then called Mack and told him that he should come in to the office when he finished up with the crime scene in the pasture.

It was good news to Mack when Dale told him that they'd captured Tim Olson's brother at the Baptism Towers motel. He was anxious to be involved with the questioning of the brother. The problem was, before things were completed, someone from animal control arrived. He was pulling a horse trailer.

"I'm here to pick up the killer horse," he said.

"Not going to happen," Mack told him. "So you'd best be hauling your ass out of here. As far as I'm concerned, you're trespassing on my property. You don't leave, and I'll arrest you."

"I have a court order to pick up the animal. It is too dangerous to have creatures like that around. That horse killed someone. It is imperative that it be dealt with as soon as possible."

"Look," Mack said, trying to be reasonable, "the horse was only trying to help his friend and defend himself. He's not a killer and doesn't deserve any of this kind of bullshit. So there's no way you're ever going to know which horse it is you're looking for."

"If you don't tell me, I'll be forced to go get some more help and a trailer big enough to take all of the horses here. If that doesn't convince you to tell us which horse is the guilty one, odds are, they'll all be put down."

"That's never going to happen. Now get the hell out of here."

When Mack told Lisa, Wanda, and Roy what was going on, they were all extremely angry. But it didn't take Roy long to come up with a way to beat the system. The other three listened intently as he told them his plan. A few minutes later, he and Wanda returned to his house.

At the same time, Lisa went to the machine shed and got the tractor with the backhoe. She immediately dug a grave for her horse, Lancer, at the edge of the pasture they were in. She was expert at using the machine, but this night it was made difficult with her eyes filled with tears. Their flow didn't abate at all until her beloved horse rested securely in its grave.

It was only minutes later that Roy and Wanda drove up to the pasture gate pulling a four horse trailer with four horses in it. As soon as it was unloaded and the new horses were safely settled in, Roy and

Wanda left. At this point, Mack called Dale to tell him he would be late getting to the office.

"What's the problem?" Dale asked. "It's not like you to be late for something this important."

"I know, Dale. But right now we've got something more important to do. It concerns saving a horse from dying for the technicalities of the law. So if you have too, start without me. I won't be in until this is finished."

Being the decent person he was, Dale answered, "I fully understand, Mack. Take whatever time you need. We can nail the creature in the cell later."

Mack and Lisa stayed in or near the place where Tim Olson murdered Lisa's horse, until everyone else finished their duties and left. After that, they were only at the gate when Roy and Wanda returned with another load of horses. There were close to thirty of them in the pasture when they finished.

"I know," said Roy, "that it would have been much easier to take Dare to someone else's place and keep him hidden there, but that would have gotten someone else directly involved. This way, none of our friends are involved. No one can go after them about any of this."

"We agree, Roy," Lisa answered. "The fewer people involved, the better. I doubt the animal control people will like it much, but as far as I'm concerned, that's tough."

And that's exactly what they thought about what they were facing when the control bunch returned. They pulled up to the now locked horse pasture gate with a stock trailer large enough to haul away all of the horses that were in the pasture on their previous visit.

"What the hell are you trying to prove here, Thomas?" Asked the control person who was the one there earlier.

"Nothing, The horse that killed the murderer is dead. He's buried over on the far side of the pasture. I'll show you his grave."

"If the horse is buried, how are we supposed to know it's the right one?"

"Because I said it was."

"Hell, we don't even know there's a horse buried there. You'll just have to dig it up for us. Fire up that backhoe of yours and have at it."

"Not in a million years. You want it dug up, you do it."

"That's fine. I'm a certified backhoe operator, so I can make short work of this with that backhoe of yours."

"Not with my backhoe you won't."

"You mean you are actually make me go get one?"

"No, because going to all that trouble will be a waste of time. I won't allow you inside that pasture with heavy machinery of any kind. You want that horse dug up, you'll have to do it with a shovel. And I'll only allow one of you to dig in that pasture at a time. To do anymore than that, we'll have to go to court to settle the issue. And I guaranty that by the time it's all said and done, the media will have made a circus of it all."

"Okay then, Thomas, we'll just have to get enough stock trailers here to haul everyone of those horses away."

"You go right ahead and do that. But since most of those horses don't belong to us, and since most of them weren't here when that murderer died, you're going to look awful foolish when the multimillion dollar lawsuits start rolling in."

"You're a real asshole, do you know that, Thomas?"

"No, I'm just a man who knows right from wrong. Something you so obviously don't know or care about."

"It's me doing the right thing. I'm following the law."

"No, it's you using the law to try to throw your weight around. And I'm damn tired of listening to you and putting up with your bullshit. Leave, or I will arrest you for trespassing. I'm still wearing a badge, and now it's you breaking the law."

"We'll see about that, Thomas. Before this day is over, I will have that badge of your's. And before I'm done, the badge of that little wife of yours too."

Mack couldn't help it. He laughed. It was a line he'd heard from so many petty little official types that he'd lost count of them years before. Lisa, who'd been listening to the conversation, reached her limit when Mack started to laugh. She walked up to about three inches from the man, looked him in the eye, and raised her hand until it was less than an inch from his face. She lifted her middle finger.

"That," she said, "is exactly how much you scare us. Now get the hell off our property before *I* arrest you."

"You bet, lady. That's something I'd really like to see you try."

Mack stopped laughing. "No, twit, you wouldn't. Now get the hell out of here before you really piss her off. You do that, and you'll be in a world of hurt when you do."

The two men with him got into their truck. "We're leaving. You can come with us or walk. It's up to you."

Grudgingly, he got into the truck. The driver of the truck stuck his head out the window and said, "It's not likely we'll be back."

CHAPTER 25

Tired as they were, Mack and Lisa went into the office after the animal control people left. They called Dale to let him know they were coming, so Craig Olson was in the interview room when they got there. A detective from the state police, Dale, and Paul were waiting for them.

After they were introduced to the detective, the first thing he said was, "So the animal control people wanted your horse? Did they get him?"

"No, they didn't. And they won't. Killing a damn good horse because you think something is absolute, only because it's a law, is not only stupid, it's insane. It doesn't seem to matter what an organization is or is supposed to do, you've always got at least one to turn the good of it into something bad."

"That's true, but do you really believe that's your decision? Shouldn't things like that be decided by a judge?"

"Sometimes, maybe. Not in this case though. To start with, how much does your average judge know about horses? There's also the horse himself. Why should he be put through that much trauma just to satisfy some jackasses idea of how each and every law should be handled?"

"Some of what you say might be true, but the stuff about putting the horse through a lot of trauma is pure nonsense. A horse doesn't know from nothing when it comes to trauma."

Mack gave the man a pained smile. There wasn't much else he could do, given he knew it would be a bad idea to deck the detective because of his complete ignorance about animals. Especially horses.

So he told him, "There's no point in us discussing this. You obviously don't know anything about horses, or probably any kind of animal, so whatever your opinion is, it's going to be wrong."

The detective pulled his head back, shocked by Mack's answer and attitude. He was used to and expected total respect from someone as lowly as a sheriff's deputy. "Now you listen to me, you can't talk…"

Dale stepped in. "Mack's right. End of discussion. It's time we got to the reason we're all here. And that's to question and hopefully get some answers from Craig Olson."

Paul also spoke up. "I agree with Dale. It's time we got to it."

"Good," Dale said. "And I think that you detective, along with Paul, who is also a detective, should start the questioning him. Mack, Lisa, or I, will step in or assist if or when needed. We definitely want to wear him down, so the odds are that we will get involved at some point."

As they expected, Craig wasn't at all forthcoming with answers of any value as the interrogation started. Things improved very little as the late night moved into morning. After the first couple of hours of questioning, Dale and Mack frequently switched with the two detectives in the room. They were a discouraged bunch by the time the sun started to rise.

Lisa, who was patiently waiting her chance since the questioning started, finally spoke up. "I know that you haven't asked me to help with this because I'm female, and you guys just don't think us women are capable of doing this, but now I want to try."

"Are you sure, Lisa?" Mack, who was one of the two men out of the interview room then, asked. "We didn't say anything earlier, because we didn't think you'd want to. You've already been through a lot, losing Lancer and all, so we didn't want to push you."

"Whatever it is you thought is fine. But now I want to give it a try. I've been watching him all night, and I think I know what has a good chance to get him talking."

"Go ahead," Mack said, "it sure can't get any worse. And knowing you, it just might get better with you in there."

When Lisa went into the room, it was Dale who stayed in there with her.

"What's the bitch doing in here?" Craig asked. "All she's gonna do is piss me off. She'll get no answers from me."

Lisa smiled at his reaction. Piss him off is exactly what she wanted to do. "So, you're afraid of women," Lisa immediately taunted him. "Watching you trying so hard to be macho when you answered questions during the night, I figured you would be." She gave him her broadest smile. "It's so much fun dealing with little boys like you, dressed up like men. Does it make you feel all grown up to rape and murder little girls?"

"I didn't rape nobody, Bitch."

"Oh, how did it go down then? You couldn't get it up as usual, so your brother did the rape and you did the murder?"

"You don't know a damn thing. If I was alone with you, you'd soon know what I can do. I get it up just fine."

"If you were alone with me, and had been for more than five minutes, someone would have called the paramedics already. And they'd have to get here quick, just to keep you alive."

Dale, seeing what Lisa was doing, couldn't resist adding to Craig's anger. "That's right," he said, poking a finger at Craig. "If we let her loose in here with you it would be a pain in the ass cleaning your blood off the walls. I've been a cop long enough to know what a chickenshit little twerp you are."

"One thing wrong with what you said, Dale. You called him chickenshit. You shouldn't do that. Even shit has some value. Little creep rapists like him don't have any value of any kind for anybody."

Craig's anger was beginning to take control. "I didn't rape nobody," he yelled this time. "I ain't never needed to rape no one neither."

"Maybe that's true," Lisa said. "But if is, it's only because you don't know how. People like you don't ever know how, unless their momma gives them hands on lessons. Did you momma forget you at lesson time?"

Craig glared at her, then talked with gritted teeth. "I'll kill you for talking about my mother that way," he threatened.

"Really? And how do you propose to do that? You're locked up here, and here is where we intend to keep you locked up. Odds are, locked up somewhere in Minnesota is where you're going to spend the rest of your life."

Craig's emotional control was gone now. All he could think of was how badly he wanted to hurt Lisa. He couldn't though, so he did the next best thing. He did what he was sure would scare the hell out of her. He warned her of what was coming.

"I've listened to you enough," he hissed, spit running out the sides of his mouth. "All you people here, in this town, in this county, ain't none of you smart enough to know what's coming. When we get done, you're going to see ruin like you never even dreamed of. We're coming down on you like the wrath of God."

"Gosh," Lisa said, her voice mocking him, "that sounds so icky scary. I suppose I should run and hide from you. And of course, the army you must have. What's it made up of, tin soldiers? I doubt that there's any real people in your life who would waste their energy helping the likes of you."

"My family has more power than you'll ever be able to imagine. They'll soon have me out of here. And once I am, we're going destroy you. This department won't exist anymore. There's no way you can stop us either. And then, bitch, you're going to be all mine."

"Do you mean that family down there in Georgia is going to come up here and rescue you so you can kill us? And then you're going to attack me all by yourself." She looked him in the eye and laughed.

"You damn right they are," he fumed. You and everyone who gets in the way. You people have interfered with our business too many times. We knew that before my brother and I ever came up here. We are going to wipe you out."

Lisa's smile was genuine this time. "Well, thank you Mister Craig Olson. You just told me what I came in here to find out. It was certainly nice of you." She couldn't resist one last dig at his ego. "Now that we're done with you, you can go back in your cell. Maybe if you work at it while you're there, you'll be able to figure out how to make that little thing in your pants do something."

Dale laughed at her words. His good humor was infectious and soon her laughter followed his.

"You're dead," Craig screamed. "You're all going to be very very dead."

Lisa decided to stick it to him one more time. She moved her face close enough to his so he could feel her breath when she talked. "It's like this, tough guy," she told him, "the truth is, it's your family who is going down. We are ready for them. You and they are losers. You always have been and you always will be."

"You're dead, you're dead…" he screamed as they dragged him to his cell.

CHAPTER 26

Barry Olson slammed his fist down on the arm of the overstuffed chair he sat in. "They got both of them?" he asked. "How the hell did they get both of them?"

"I'm not totally sure," Jeff Olson, Barry's oldest son answered. "But from what I do know, whatever it was that went wrong, it started with Tim. Craig should have known better than to bring him along."

"I know, but he was just trying to help out his brother."

"Really?" Jeff frowned. "How? Tim never was much good for nothing. It's starting to look like Craig isn't either."

"That's a hell of a way to talk about your brothers. Make mistakes or not, they were still trying to look out for family. Something you don't seem to be doing much of right now."

"That ain't fair, what you just said. I look out for family. I just don't do stupid things like Craig and Tim did in Minnesota."

"Do you really think you could have done that much better than what they did? Seems like there isn't anybody who's had any success with those people up there in Clayborne County, Minnesota."

"Could be you've been sending the wrong people to deal with the situation. You send the right ones, you might get some better results."

"And who might that be? You?"

"That's right. Me. You send me, things will get done."

"I've been sending the best of the best, Jeff. Some of those men who died or are now in jail were with us for many years, and served us well the whole time. I can't see where you could do any better."

"Of course you can't. You never give me a chance to try."

"Maybe not, but there's a reason for it."

"And that is?"

"I don't trust you to hold it together. You've got a temper that won't quit. You're forever flying off about one thing or another. You go up there and get into a skirmish, then lose that temper of yours, you'll end up in deep shit. Worse than that, you'll bring down those you're with. The people who trusted you to do the right thing."

"Won't happen," Jeff argued. "I only get pissed at the stupid shit that goes on around here. I get into it with them people up there, I won't get pissed, I'll get busy. And I mean the kind of busy that involves the killing of the lot of them."

"You really think you can get the job done? The job Craig went up there to gather info on?"

"Damn right. But you got to let me do it my way."

"What's that? The same old thing? That's been done about every time and it hasn't worked yet."

"That I know all too well. But Craig's idea, even if it might work, will take too many men and too much time."

"So, what's your idea?"

"I want to go up there with more men than we used before, but not so many as Craig's plan would take. Then I want to hit them hard, where it'll hurt them the most."

"You must be planning on going after the sheriff's department direct to break your brother out of his jail cell."

"No, I don't. The sheriff's department will come later. I'm going to take out those Thomases first. They always seem to be the catalyst that brings everything and everyone together. We take them out of the picture, and I believe the rest up there will pretty much fall apart."

"You plan on killing the bunch of them then?"

"All but one. I'm going to try to keep that Lisa bitch Craig told us about alive. Then we can use her for bait, to get Craig out without having a gun battle that could cost us men we'll need."

"What if you can't keep that bitch alive, Jeff? Then what?"

"If we can't manage that with her, we'll do our best to keep one of the other two Thomas bitches alive. If we can't, we'll get Craig out some other way."

Barry shook his head. "I don't know. I've been half thinking about going up there myself. Back in the early days, I was always the one to get us out of trouble, when there was trouble."

It was Jeff's turn to shake his head. He put his hand on Berry's shoulder. "That was a very long time ago, dad. It was different then and you were young. Not to mention, you mostly bribed your way through the bulk of our law problems. Ain't that way now. For reasons what don't make any sense to me at all, no amount of money is enough to get any of them Thomases to back off and let us do our thing. So it's best if you let me handle it this time."

"As much as I hate the thought of sending the last son I have still at home and free, you might be right. Thing is though, You're going to have to give me some time to think things through. Won't be a bad idea for you, either, to use that time to go over what you've got planned, and maybe fill in the holes in it."

"I'll be doing that. The one thing I agree with Craig on. It's hard to do too much planning." He laughed. "Especially when it comes to killing a bunch of them law lovers."

"You've got the truth there, Jeff. You've got the whole truth."

CHAPTER 27

There was no doubt in anyone's mind now, that trouble was once again headed their way. Dale gave all the deputies instructions to watch every way it was possible, for groups of men coming into, or even driving through, Clayborne County.

Craig Olson was given his allowed phone call, and within hours his attorneys arrived. Two of them to start, then a third from Georgia a couple of hours later. He flew in on his own private jet, and brought his own secretary with him.

No one was sure what her actual purpose was, but from the way she held on to the attorney's arm, the people in the sheriff's office who watched them were fairly certain it wasn't clerical.

The lawyers met with Craig, then with the county prosecutor to discuss the charges against him. After a private meeting of the lawyers only, they asked for and got a bail hearing.

Even though they were very good at what they did, and made some sound arguments for his release, the judge turned them down. They just couldn't convince the judge. The charges against him were too strong.

When he was told of the results of the hearing, Craig went into a rage. This was something new to him. In Georgia his family controlled enough bought and paid for officials to never allow something like this happen. For the next ten minutes he only stopped cursing his lawyers once.

After a long string of curses, he yelled, "You tell them Thomas people, you tell them that hell is headed their way. They've screwed with us way too many times." It either didn't occur to him, or he just didn't care about it, but he should have known that it was the judge, not anyone in the Thomas family, who decided he wouldn't be released. Then, to prove how powerful and dangerous he was, he added to his tirade. "It's going to be fun watching each and every one of them die."

One of his Minnesota lawyers was by now more than simply fed up with his stupidity. Running off at the mouth the way Craig did, could only do him harm. So he told him to quiet down.

"The hell you say," Craig snarled at him. "I'll do as I choose, and if you don't like it, you can just fuck off."

"Keep it up, Craig, and I will. I see no reason to represent someone as hell bent on destroying any chance of a good defense by constantly shooting off his mouth."

"You can't quit. We own you. You are bought and paid for."

"The truth is, slavery ended in this country right after the civil war. That means you can't own me. Also, I haven't been paid as yet. So…yes, I can quit. Not only can I, that's exactly what I intend on doing." With that, he packed up his brief case and left.

The other Minnesota lawyer knew then that if Craig didn't calm down he was going to get himself convicted of the entire long list of crimes he was charged with. So that's what he told him.

"Well, you can stick that bullshit right up your ass," Craig growled at him. "I'm entitled to say what I want to say."

"You intend to continue running off at the mouth then?"

"You damn right I do."

"Even if I tell you I will quit if you do?"

Craig grinned this time. He wasn't worried. Lawyers were a dime a dozen, and what they did was always about money, nothing else. So he flippantly said, "Go ahead, quit. It won't matter."

So a second lawyer left. His Georgia lawyer wanted to at that point, but knew that for him it was impossible. If he did, the repercussions in Georgia would be too serious to contemplate. Like it or not, he was stuck with Craig.

But he did tell him, "You just got rid of the two best defense attorneys in Minnesota. The only other one in the state as good as he is, already turned us down. So you've done a great deal toward getting yourself convicted."

"Don't matter. I won't be here for no trial. They'll be coming here to get me out of this jail. Which they will. And while they're here, they'll for sure kill everyone of those damned Thomases. This jail, this whole sheriff's department, will follow."

"Do you really think you can kill that many people and get away with it?"

"No problem. They'll all be dead, so there won't be any witnesses."

"What about me?"

"You're my lawyer. You can't tell on me. What I say is privileged."

"If you say so."

The Georgia lawyer left then. He knew that what Craig told him about killing so many people wasn't privileged. In this case, because lives were actually in danger, he was obligated to report what Craig said. So this time, even after being corrupted for so many years by his association with the Olson family, he reported it.

He asked for and got a meeting with the county prosecutor. There, he told the prosecutor what Craig told him. Then he returned to his motel room to wait for the disaster he knew was coming. The only saving grace was the compliant secretary he brought with him. He never did find out if she knew even enough to type, but she was a wonderfully willing time filler either way.

The prosecutor, however, didn't have any of that kind of luxury. His wife, now sixty, had lost all interest in any of that kind of activity two years previously. So without any kind of break he called Dale, and as soon as he answered the phone, he gave Dale a detailed explanation of what Craig's lawyer told him.

"I appreciate you calling me with this information. It's going to, I'm sure, save some lives. But why did the lawyer give it to you?"

"He was required to. Threats like that can't be kept secret. They're too dangerous. So by law, they have to be reported."

"We were expecting them to try something with us. We just weren't sure what it would be. Now we know. It gives us a much better chance of defending ourselves."

"That's good, Dale. Let me know if there's anything more I can do."

"I will do that."

It was getting late in the day, so Dale set up a meeting for the next morning. He requested that all deputies possible attend. For those who couldn't be there in the morning, he set up a meeting for the late afternoon. Then he contacted Mack.

"Will it be possible for you and the rest of your family to meet with me in the next hour or so?"

"It should be, if there's a good reason. Mind telling me what's going on?"

"Not at all. I'll explain it in detail when we get together later. For now, what I want to talk to all of you about is keeping you alive."

"Keeping us alive? Are you serious? What's the problem that you think you have to do something special to keep us alive?"

"You are the first and priority target of the Olson family. They plan on hitting you harder than anyone in the past has ever done. I think it would be a good idea if I could go over everything with all of you. You've got an incredibly competent family, Mack, but even you guys can do better if you know what's coming."

"You are for sure right about that. What time and where. We'll all be there."

Dale told him, and as soon as they hung up, Mack started calling. Everyone instantly agree. Everyone but Roy. He asked some questions before he would agree. That didn't surprise Mack.

"Why the hell are all of us the targets of those people. I don't wish this on you and Lisa by any stretch, but wouldn't it make more sense if it was just you and Lisa they were after? You're the ones who've been raising the most hell with them."

"It seems as though their vendetta against us goes way back. They started out here in Minnesota, and they've been involved in about every kind of crime there is, for a very long time. And all of you, at one time or another, have been involved with me, and lately Lisa, in dealing with those crimes. So they're pissed at all of us."

"I guess, but it seems there's more to it that just that."

"I think there is. We're a symbol. We stand for what's right, and against what's wrong. We've consistently stood up against them and all those like them."

"That all? It still doesn't seem like enough."

"We also aren't afraid of them. They hate that the most. They operate on fear. Our lack of it can sometimes inspire others to stand up to them. That is something they absolutely cannot afford."

"Okay, I see what you're saying. I'll be at the meeting."

Before Dale got the chance to say anything when they met, Roy told them, "One thing we have to consider is where they will stay when they first get here. This time, I don't think they'll be staying in Jackstone County. It's too obvious, after all that's happened They know we'll be watching everything going on there real close."

"Where do you think they'll stay?" Dale asked.

"I can't say for sure, but if it was me, it would be at Lands Magnificent. Normally, that would be the last place you would look for them."

"I don't know?" Dale questioned. "Wouldn't they stick out like a sore thumb there."

Mack, who now realized how logical Roy's idea was, now commented on it. "Actually, it's the one place where they can blend in. One of the major reasons the Lands Magnificent Resort has done so well is because of the conventions they've managed to attract. Especially smaller ones that a lot of places don't much care to deal with."

"Do you really think those hoodlums can pretend to be some kind of convention?"

"If not that, Dale, they will be able to come across as some kind of legitimate group. The resort gets a lot of that type of activity too. And that way, they can come anyway they want to. As singles, or any number up to five or six without attracting too much attention."

"They could probably do it without attracting any attention. And other than us looking for them, they likely won't attract any attention."

"I don't know. Do you really think they'll want to stay that close to us?"

"I do," Mack said. "Being close will save them that fairly long drive when they're ready to attack us. A short drive will increase the chances of it being a surprise. Not to mention that when they get here, they'll be able to go to the resort without driving through Kingsburg. Another way to keep from being noticed."

"What you two are saying makes a lot of sense. But now comes the big problem. Because of the way the resort is designed, it's going to be near impossible to watch close enough to know for sure they actually are staying there."

"It won't be near as tough as it seems. I know where we can get a lot of help."

"How are you going to manage that, Mack?" Dale asked. "We're going to have to be careful about who we let get involved in this sort of thing."

"I'll talk to Rodney Twilabee about it. He's the CEO there, and he's helped us out in the past. I know that we'll never be able to call him Saint Rodney, but he keeps his word, so we can trust him."

"What can he realistically help with? He's not the kind of man who has time to watch people check in."

"No, but he can legitimately review the daily checkin logs and let us know about any strange activity. It might not solve the entire problem, but it will help."

"Something else he can do," Roy added. "He can keep an eye on the reservations. They get a bunch of new reservations, especially from Georgia with a short lead time, we can keep an eye on who made them after they get here."

"Okay," Dale agreed. "You've convinced me." He looked at Mack. "Are you going to call Twilabee?"

"I will, yes." It was the first thing he did when their meeting was over.

Twilabee listened intently until Mack finished explaining the situation. "You're sure, Mack, that things are that serious. Those people are actually going to try and hunt your whole family down and kill you?"

"I don't have the slightest doubt. And after us, the sheriff's department. the town, and then everything on the outskirts of town which has any value."

"So you're saying that they'll even eventually go after Lands Magnificent."

Mack paused for a moment before answering. He hadn't thought at all about the resort being part of what was going on. But now that he was, he could see the irony and the humor in the idea. The resort was one of the things that occurred during his lifetime that he most hated. But he'd managed to make peace with the thought of its existence, and had something of a friendship with Twilabee. Those facts, however, didn't change the truth. And that truth was, Mack would probably find his own kind of delight in watching the end of the resort.

Because of all that, Mack hedged his answer. "It is a possibility. I don't have any idea though, how likely it is that it will happen. So I can't use that as an excuse for asking for your help."

"Anybody else, and I'd have my suspicions. But not with you. And the truth is, I want to help, regardless of their plans for the resort."

"Good. You'll help keep an eye out for them then."

"I'll do even more than that, Mack. Starting tonight, I'll be looking at all reservations and the checkin log. Both morning and night. I see anything at all suspicious and I'll give you a call."

"Thanks, Rodney. I really appreciate this one."

"No problem. You'd do the same for me."

With Rodney's promise of help, Mack felt as if a great weight was lifted off his shoulders. So much so, that he thought it would be a good idea to spend some time with Lisa, away from the job. He knew that this might be the last chance for a while. She didn't argue when he called her to tell her they were taking the following morning off.

CHAPTER 28

Mack told Lisa that he was going to spend a little while that evening going over their bank accounts, just to be sure they were in order. What he really did was look up horses for sale.

He knew that most people would consider it too soon for her to get another horse, but Mack felt otherwise. For most people, the quickest way to ease the hurt of the loss of an animal who has been a long time friend is to get another one.

Another thing people often believed was that if you replaced your loyal companion too soon, you dishonor the one you lost. He felt the opposite. The sooner you brought a new one into your life, the sooner that individual would begin to get the kind of treatment only you could give.

The next morning, after breakfast with the family, Mack and Lisa started their day. Mack still hadn't told her what he was up to, so she was surprised when he stopped at a small horse ranch.

"Why are we here, Mack?" she asked.

"I thought we'd look at some horses. You've been without one of your own long enough."

"I don't know. How can I replace Lancer so soon? It doesn't seem right."

"To start with, Lisa, you won't be replacing him. You can't replace him. What you're doing when you get another one is bringing someone new into your life. That doesn't mean you want to push out the memories of what you had in the past."

"I'm still not sure, Mack."

"I understand. But it won't hurt to look, will it?"

"I guess not, but don't be mad at me if I don't find any that I want today."

"I won't. It might take a few months and several times out looking before you decide on one. That's fine with me. But I think it is time to start looking. More than that though, I just wanted this extra time alone with you. We need more of that."

"I know, and I think we're both overdue in trying to make it happen."

Mack smiled at her comment. He loved to hear her say things like that, because he it meant they had the same strong feelings.

When the owner of the ranch met them at the main corral, he asked who the horse was for. When they told him he said, "I assume you want a gentle animal. And maybe one not too large."

Lisa shook her head in disgust. This was an all too common reaction to her. She was slim, and a little less than average in size. On top of that there was the feature that clinched the attitude of most men. She was beautiful, and therefore helpless. No one who looked as good as she did, could be strong too.

She gave the man her best smile anyway. "I'm not concerned about the horse's size. As far as gently goes, I want one with plenty of life left in it. What I'd really like is a spirited one that is well trained in the basics. Do you have anything like that? If you do, I want to see your best."

What he brought her was an okay horse, but one with little of what she wanted. "I hope that wasn't what you'd call your best," she said, "because he missed the mark by quite a lot."

"I've only got one better. I didn't bring him out because he's still young, and isn't much beyond green broke."

"And you don't believe I can handle him?" She looked at Mack, and her expression showed how little she thought of the rancher's ideas. She turned back to the rancher. "It's up to you. If you want even the slightest chance of selling me a horse, you'll bring him out."

It was obvious he didn't like the idea, but he brought out the horse. Lisa led him by his halter to see how he was to handle. She managed him without any problem, so she told the rancher, "Put a saddle on him, so I can take him for a short ride."

The horse was a bit tense and nervous when she mounted him, but he calmed within a few steps. Lisa put him through his paces, then dismounted.

"He's a good horse," she said. "And I will definitely keep him in consideration. And thank you for letting me try him out."

The rancher was looking at her differently now. "You're welcome," he smiled. "And I have to tell you, I've never seen him react before, the way he did with you. You certainly do have the right touch."

"I've been riding since I was a small kid, so I guess I should know something."

"It showed," he said.

They told the man there was a good chance he would see them again, and left the place. As they drove out, Lisa was saddened by the rundown look of the place. All of the buildings were in obvious need of repair, the fences were almost as bad, and even the gravel driveway was full of potholes and badly in need of grading. It made her wonder about the place in general. The horse especially. If the place itself was this neglected, what kind of care were the horses getting.

The next place they stopped, the buildings, fences, and driveway were all in excellent shape. The horses, however, were not. There were ten of them. Six were old, and in all around terrible shape. Three of the last four were somewhat better, but had hooves that needed trimming, and hadn't been brushed for a very long time.

The last one looked better, but carried the signs of mistreatment. She was skittish, and carried a look that warned against turning your back on her. Do it on one end and she'd kick. Do it on the other, and she'd happily bite. Even with those faults, Lisa was confident that with the right training in huge doses, the horse had potential. But with the busy schedule they had, it would be more than she and Mack could do a proper job of.

The next three stops were show places. Everything about them in near perfect order, and all the horses well cared for. The problem again was the men who operated two of them. One look at Lisa and they were sure she couldn't handle much of a horse.

At one place, the man reluctantly let her ride a couple of the horses, but none of the spirited ones. The other man refused to let her ride any of his horses.

The woman who operated the ranch that was as nice as any of them, let Lisa ride any horse she wanted too. There were three possibles on their list when they left the place.

The last visit left them feeling near sick over what they found. The place was literally falling apart. The horses there were in even worse condition. There was even a dead horse in the small pasture. A pasture so over grazed that there was barely enough grass for one horse, so it couldn't possibly feed the dozen or so horses on it who were desperately looking for something to eat.

As they drove home, Mack asked her, "What did you think about the day? Was it at all productive for you?"

"In some ways, yes. In other ways, not at all. I've lived in this area all my life, and I never before realized there was so much cruelty toward horses going on."

"Most of places we stopped, they seemed to be trying, at least, to take care of the animals."

"I know. But there should be a place where some of the worst could be taken care of. No living creature, no matter what breed or species, should ever have to live the hell some of them we saw today are going through."

"I agree, Lisa. "I'd even consider trying to take care of some of them, but it just wouldn't work on our land. When we set up the place, we only set aside enough space for the horses we already had. Adding more then the one you're going to eventually get would just be a good start to overcrowding them."

"I know that, Mack. I know there's not much we can do, especially since our days are already filled with trying to make things better. But I'll still keep wishing someone would do something."

"So will I. And to tell you the truth, what I'm wishing for now is a nap."

Lisa grinned. "What kind of nap? You wouldn't actually thinking about one of those naps where you do something silly like sleep, would you?"

Mack returned her grin. "I'm going to give Dale a call. If there's nothing big going on, I think we'll take the rest of the day off."

Lisa was already in bed, under the covers, when he finished talking to Dale. He undressed, then crawled in with her. It was almost an hour later when they slept.

There was still some afternoon when they got out of bed, so Mack suggested a walk in the wildlife refuge. To the eyes of a lot of people, it still looked like a burned out wasteland. To the experienced eyes of Lisa and Mack, it was once again a beautiful wild place. Well over a year had gone by since it burned, and the recovery it was making illustrated the positive power of nature in a way little else could do.

Nearly all the trees were lost in the fire. Those burned out relics still standing were a stark contrast to the wealth of lifeforms growing beneath them. Various seedlings were now in abundance. New bushes of several varieties were scattered throughout the refuge. Most of the spring flowers had bloomed and gone, but there were enough summer blooming plants to provide patches of color that generously filled the meadows.

More that anything, in every niche possible, native grasses grew in many shades of vivid green. It was a summer of more than adequate rain, and that along with the extra fertility provided from the ashes of the fire, the grasses not only grew prolifically. They grew strong and tall.

As they looked around them at all the life in every direction, they remembered the fire. It was a wall of flames, in places over a hundred feet in the air, that destroyed everything caught in its path. Fighting that fire, working with the crews trying mightily to bring it under control, they could never have dreamed they would see what they were seeing now.

Lisa held Mack's hand as they walked, and often when they stopped to look at something, she rested her head against him. When she did, he wrapped his arm around her, and was filled with a feeling of total contentment. Here he was, out in the refuge so full of life that felt as if it were a second home, his arms around a woman he'd never quite feel as though he was good enough for. He was a lucky man and he knew it. Then he got even luckier.

They were standing next to a pond, in some low ground. The land to the north rose up somewhat over a couple hundred feet rather steeply, so they couldn't see far in that direction. Then what happened next shocked both of them.

Suddenly appearing over the rise were two black noses, followed by the bear cubs who owned them. Not far behind the cubs was mama. She stopped at the top of the hill, her nose in the air for a moment. Then she lowered her head and stared at them.

Very softly, Lisa said to Mack, "I can't hardy believe this. Do you think she's the same one we saw before?"

"Probably. I don't really think we'd get two different mother bears in this short a time, in an area as settled as this one has become."

"Next question. Do you think she'll ignore us again. I sure would hate to have to shoot her."

The bear growled then, but the sound of it wasn't much like it would have been if she was angry. It was more like she was telling them she was there, and that they should take that into consideration if they so much as moved.

Mack and Lisa were smart enough to take her advice, and stood as still as possible. They felt reasonably safe as long as the cubs didn't get too close. But the cubs, being young and loving to play, decided tag would now be a good game to play.

They chased each other in ever widening circles, until one of them did exactly what Mack and Lisa didn't want them to do. It ran behind them, which put them between the cub and mama. She shook her head, growling again, loud enough to be heard a long way away.

Mack and Lisa took out their guns, hoping against hope that they wouldn't need to use them. But they quickly feared they would, as mama slowly started down the hill toward them. Lisa lifted her weapon, pointed it at mama, then looked at Mack as if to ask the question, "Should I shoot now."

Mack shook his head no. Watching the way the bear moved, he was fairly confident she wasn't going to attack. If that was her intention, he was sure she would have charged down the hill. Not walk slowly down it. Even so, he kept his gun in his hand, which was down at his side.

She continued watching them as she grew closer to them, but didn't seem overly concerned about them. As she gradually moved around them, she caught up with the careless cub. She gave him a low growl, as if she was scolding him. when he appeared to ignore her, she gave him a light swat across his rear, then continued to walk away from them.

Lisa and Mack gave an audible sigh as they watched her saunter away.

"Sometimes," Lisa said, "things are almost impossible to believe, even when you're watching them."

"That one wasn't just near impossible to believe, according to the books, it wasn't supposed to be possible at all. It's something that's incredibly rare. We were lucky to be able to be part of something like that."

"I agree, Mack. It was scary as hell, but something I wouldn't have wanted to miss."

They were a contented pair when they went home that night. In the morning, they woke up with the good feelings they took to bed with them. That changed when Roy told them about the lead story on the local TV station.

Two teenage boys, who had gone into the refuge with twenty-two rifles to shoot what ever they could, were found mauled by what they said was a mama bear with two cubs. When questioned, they admitted that they were shooting at the bear cubs. It wasn't until they wounded one of the cubs that the mama bear tore into them.

At that point, Mack and Lisa vowed to go to work in defense of the bear. The boys were completely wrong, and they saw no reason for the bear to be the one to pay for their sins.

CHAPTER 29

It was midmorning when Mack got the call from Rodney Twilabee. "It looks like it's started. Last night, the men from Georgia began arriving. There were four in the first bunch. Two in the second, six in the third, and four each in the last two. From what the night clerk said, they were all well dressed. Each group arrived in a dark colored, late model SUV. All were on the high end, price wise. Their rooms are all on the same floor in the same section."

"That's about what we figured. And given there are twenty of them, they must really be planning on raising a lot of hell."

"It sure does appear that way. What do you want us to do now?"

"Without being obvious, keep the best eye on them you can. The last thing I want to do is bring any of this down on your head."

"I think I already knew that, Mack. I'll put my security people on it. They're used to keeping a low profile. How often do you want me to fill you in on their activities."

"As often as they're active. And especially if they all become active at the same time."

"We can do that. I'll be talking to you."

Mack immediately called Dale to tell him the latest. They set up a meeting timed for the end of first shift. At that time, they intended to have only three deputies in the field. That way, all of first shift and most of second were able to attend the meeting.

Dale, Mack, Lisa, and Paul had already drawn up a plan to deal with the invaders from Georgia. That meant the meeting only consisted of a review of the plan with everyone, then detailed explanations of each persons duty when the action started.

The first part of their plan was to use Craig Olson as bait to draw out as many of the Georgians as possible. They had already started the spread of a rumor about moving Craig to a more secure location in Minneapolis, He was to be moved late in the evening, taking a route using back roads so they could initially avoid notice.

In reality, they had no intention of moving Craig, so when it came time to make the move, they loaded a deputy the same size and shape as Craig into the back of one of their cars. He went into the car with handcuffs on, but they were immediately removed.

Three cars left the rear of the sheriff's office, with the imposter for Craig in the middle car. Everyone in the procession knew the route well, so they knew the best location for the Georgians to ambush the sheriff's caravan. It was also a perfect place to setup a trap for the Georgians. Dale and his people were fairly sure they'd be faced with a sudden blockade made by two of the SUVs the Georgians arrived in at Lands Magnificent. They also assumed that somewhat over half of the twenty men would be their reception committee.

Every person from the sheriff's department who was there wore body armor. None of the men planning on breaking Craig Olson free wore any. They were sure that when they had the sheriff's people stopped, and blocked both front and back by their SUVs, they would be forced to surrender. At which time they would be executed.

They, of course, were wrong. As soon as they moved in on the sheriff's cars, a voice called out from the dark telling them to halt. They responded with a hail of bullets in the direction of the voice. The deputies in the cars quickly bailed out, and laid down a rain of bullets on the Georgians. More, even heavier fire, came from the darkness.

Everyone from the sheriff's department had earlier been briefed about who and what kind of men they were in a gun battle with. So there was little hesitation when they fired. They did as they were trained to do, and as much as possible aimed at the chest, the largest target.

The gun battle lasted less than five minutes. As soon as the firing stopped, the body count started. Of the original twelve men that were still alive, Craig's brother Jeff was one. His still bleeding chest wound was serious, but he did have a chance of recovery. The other surviver dropped to the ground the instant the shooting started, but was hit in his shoulder and his side. His wounds were also serious, but life threatening only if his bleeding wasn't stopped soon. Ten of the men were dead. Two deputies were wounded, neither of them seriously.

After a quick survey of the situation, Dale told the deputies who had already volunteered to go, to immediately head for the Thomas ranch, where a second attack was expected to start at any time.

Because everyone was sure there would be an assault on the caravan that the Georgians thought carried Craig, most of the force of Dale and his deputies were at that location. Only three were at the Thomas's, along with Mack and the rest of his family. Since she was considered part of the family, Sue Sartor was with them too. Not that she would have it any other way. As was the force that met the bunch on the back road, everyone in the Thomas group wore armor.

Mack wasn't certain which direction the attack would come from, so he decided to set up his defenses close to home. The first thing he, Ben, and Roy did was set up a series of lights. Some were on the ground and some were in trees, but when they were all on, they lit up the area like it was daylight. He could also operate them remotely.

Each person in their group was stationed someplace above ground level. That gave them a wider range of view. They were all in their stations, waiting for the men who thought they would be facing easy targets. They were sure that Mack and Lisa would be with the cars moving Craig, and didn't consider Ben or Roy to be a problem. They were simply too old to put up much of a defense, if they could put up any at all.

What those men believed and reality were far different things. Mack and Lisa were home, were both excellent shots with any weapon, and were now armed with semiautomatic, high powered rifles. Roy was almost as good a shot as Mack, but Wanda was the best shot of the group. She was one of those people who, if she shot at something, she never failed to hit it. Ben was less proficient, so along with the rifle in his hand, he had a shotgun resting close by. Theresa could handle any gun if she was forced to, but wasn't necessarily all that accurate. So she held a twelve gauge, pump shotgun. If anyone got close enough to her, she wouldn't have to worry so much about precise accuracy. Sue Sartor wasn't proficient with any particular weapon, but felt most comfortable with the thirty/thirty lever action she held.

Two of the deputies were stationed in a wooded area just off the road. They were off in both directions, so when the eight killer's from Georgia approached the Thomases from each direction, Mack and company were warned by a prearranged signal.

Mack allowed the cars to get as close as they dared, and then let the men get out. They fanned out as they approached Ben and Theresa's house, since it was the closest to the road.

When Mack figured they were in the right position, he called out, "Drop your weapons and lie face down on the ground."

So naturally, being the super macho men they were, the killers started shooting in every direction. Mack turned on the lights. "Time to give it up," he yelled. They were startled by the light, but not smart enough to give it up.

Everyone waiting for the killers then returned fire. A couple of minutes later, the shooting stopped. All of the would be killers were on the ground. The three bleeding were the only ones still among the living.

When he called in to let Dale know what went down, and to request ambulances for the wounded, he was told that only one was available. When they arrived, they took the killer from Georgia who was in the worst condition to the hospital. He died on the operating table.

Of the two picked up later, one died on his way in. The other made it, but lost an arm. It was hit at close range by a shotgun, and there was no way the doctors could save it.

No one located at the Thomas's was injured. A few windows and some other minor damage to Ben's house was the only damage Georgians accomplished.

All Mack could think of, all he could say about what just happened was, "Stupid. So damn entirely stupid."

"I agree," Lisa said. "You'd think that as often as this kind of thing had been tried against us, that they'd know better."

"That would require some intelligence," Mack said. "The men who were here were anything but. And the people who hired them, well, they might be clever enough to kidnap innocent women, but intelligent, I don't hardly think so."

"But at least," Lisa said, "it should be over with this bunch now."

"Don't count on it," Mack answered. "The head of this clan is still alive, and he has to be dealt with, one way or the other.'

Lisa gave him a grim smile. "And I don't guess there's any doubt who is going to do that job. Would there, Mack?"

Mack's answer included a frown. "No, Lisa," he said, "there sure isn't. And knowing you as well as I do, I expect you will want to be in on it with me."

"This time, no, I don't want to. That's not going to keep me out of it though. I'm about as sick of all this killing as I could get, but I couldn't live with myself if I didn't see this to its end."

"So we feel the same. We're both sick of this killing. I keep hoping that the hopeless, useless people like this latest bunch, will somehow learn. The trouble is, all of them have brain parts missing. Their brains just don't seem to be able to operate at full capacity. They simply don't have the ability to feel any kind of decency or compassion. I don't think they're capable of caring much for or about anything or anybody. Not even themselves, in most cases."

"You're right, Mack, of that I have no doubt. But I don't think the problem is only with the total trash like these human traffickers. Think about the way average people treat animals. Most people who have pets really care about them. Then you have so many whose cruelty ranges from simple neglect to outright severe cruelty."

"I know. The abuse of animals on all levels. Nothing is worse than corporate agriculture. For big agriculture, the constant, day to day cruelty would be difficult to make any worse than what it is now."

Lisa kicked the ground in disgust before she said any more. "Then you have what can only be called a miscarriage of justice. I know it's a small thing, as stuff like this goes. But that meeting they're having tomorrow, to decide whether or not to hire professional hunters to go after that mama bear and her cubs, is a travesty of the first order. That bear should no more be hunted down than you and I should."

"From my point of view," Mack answered, "killing that bear is worse than what happened to any of the dead trash around here."

"Is there anything we can do to help the bear?"

"We can go to the meeting and plead the bear's case for her. Something I fully intend to do."

Lisa finally managed a partial smile. "I was hoping you'd do that. If anyone can convince them to do the right thing, it's you."

"Don't get your hopes up, Lisa. Given the kind of people those boys are tells me what kind of parents they have. When all is said and done, the judge will allow the hunt."

"There must be something we can do."

"There is. And I'll spring it on them tomorrow."

CHAPTER 30

Barry Olson was having fits. He had just received the news about his oldest son and the infallible group of men he sent to Minnesota. They were the best of the best, and now they were all in jail, the hospital, or dead.

Those people up there in Minnesota had his three sons too. One was in jail, one in the hospital, and the third was dead. All he could do is wonder what happened. How could a bunch of hicks living in a rural county with only one town big enough to amount too much do this to him?

Here he was, in his sixties, and no longer the head of any kind of organization. All his adult life he'd run some kind of syndicate that operated outside the law. It was often a scramble to stay ahead of the legal system, but they'd always managed it in the past. Now it was all gone. And why? Only because of an overly zealous sheriff who refused to be bought, an ex-rodeo cowboy who seemed to have a special ability to dodge bullets, and his wife, a little girl who instead of arresting his people, should be home changing diapers.

He hated them, and everyone connected to them, no matter how remotely. He might be down now, but there was no doubt that he would rebuild his organization. And when he did, they were done. His priority now was revenge. Total revenge. Somehow, he would take them down. And just for spite, when the time came, he would run all branches of his new crime organization from Clayborne County. And he would make that resort, Lands Magnificent, his headquarters. That was something else he intended to steal.

First and foremost though, he definitely needed to get his sons, who were still living, free from that damn sheriff and his people. and home again. He no longer had the man power to actually break them out of jail, but he did still have a lot of cash reserve. That meant bribery was now the best option. And the best target for bribery were the right judge, along with a powerful prosecutor.

So he sat there, smoking a big cigar, while he dreamed his dreams and planned his plans. As he ran his playful fantasies through his now slipping brain, there was no way he could comprehend what going up against the likes of Dale Magee and Mack and Lisa Thomas would actually be like. He'd always had someone else do it for him.

Which for the condition he was in, it was just as well. The truth would have devastated him.

CHAPTER 31

The media learned of the two separate shootings before sunrise. Because of the number of dead, they soon were referring to the incidents as massacres. It didn't take long after that for the television people to request a news conference. They were confident that they could make Sheriff Dale Magee look like an inept fool. And doing so, would be a real treasure of reporting for them. And best of all, a ratings booster.

Almost nothing brought up their ratings the way making a good, honest man look like a fool. And nothing on earth was as important as raising the ratings. Higher ratings meant more cash. Nothing, not even honest, accurate reporting could out *trump* more cash.

Because of the number of things that needed to be done before he had the time to do it, Dale managed to hold it off until ten AM. Not wanting it to be turned into a political media circus, he only allowed Mack, Lisa, Paul, and three of his most senior deputies up on the temporary stage with him. No one up there had the time to freshen up, nor any interest in doing so, before the questions started. So, after being up all night and in a major gun battle, they all looked rough.

Dale was, and looked, exhausted, when he stood at the dais. The first question thrown at him was intentionally nasty. It was meant to soften him up.

It was given to him by a reporter who always made his questions seem more like accusations. "How in God's green earth can you justify so many dead? There had to have been a better way to deal with this."

Dale was in no mood for his kind of witch hunt and let it show with his answer. "Obviously you don't have any idea what happened, what it was about, or what caused it. There are, however, several innocent young ladies, who were kidnapped by those men, but are now home free, who do."

"You didn't answer my question. How can you…"

"You're right, I didn't. And I don't intend to. It was a stupid question that you asked only to bait me, to get me to say something wrong. I'll answer all legitimate questions today, but I will not stand here and suffer your twisted questions designed to make me and my department look bad. I don't, at the moment, care a damn about your ratings, so keep it civil."

The same reporter, "But I have a right to ask whatever I want to ask."

"You sure do. And I have the right to cancel this news conference at any time I choose too. Keep it up and I will."

That was enough for Mack. He had no doubt about Dale's ability to handle the media. He'd done if often enough in the past. But after what he'd been through the past couple of days, why should he have to. Mack was close to exhaustion himself, so he could at least understand how Dale must feel. He was the sheriff, so the pressure of organizing the department for what occurred was double for him compared to the rest of them. He was also the person responsible for it, so the stress he'd lived with went beyond what most people ever feel. And worst of all, it was obvious what the media had planned for him. They were going to try to make him the goat, so they could broadcast and write about the no good sheriff from Clayborne County. A good ratings booster.

Before another question was asked, Mack moved to the dais. A few of the right words too Dale, and he moved aside for Mack. Mack then stared out at the media people, a large frown on his face.

"I requested the sheriff to step aside because I have a few words for you people."

"We requested a news conference with the sheriff," a TV reporter said. "And that's exactly what we expect."

"You have every right to expect whatever you want to expect. That however, doesn't mean you'll get it today. If listening to me is too boring for you, then I suggest you leave and go someplace else and haunt someone else."

"I might just do that. You sure don't look like anyone who matters. And you for sure don't even look like a cop, dressed like Wyatt Earp the way you are."

His words were followed by a wave of light laughter that ran through the media bunch.

"Now you have something to report," Mack said. "You could probably produce a whole story about the deputy who didn't dress the way you expected him too. But that's enough of that kind of crap. I'm going to ask you all this once, and only once. Do you want to hear me out or not? If not, just leave. We don't need to discuss it."

Only two reporters left, and one of them didn't get far before he turned around and rejoined the group.

"Good," Mack told them, "We'll move on then. Just don't interrupt me until I finish saying what I've go to say. Until then, I won't be answering any questions."

"What if we have questions about what you're telling us?"

"Write them down. I get questions before I'm done talking, I'll shut this news conference down." He glared at the group. They finally decided to behave for a while.

Mack started his story with the abduction by Darrin Whitcomb of several young girls, which occurred the previous year, and went through all the events, shootings, and killings that happened and were related to human trafficking since it happened.

He finished with, "And that brings us to tonight. Twenty hired killers made the trip up here from Georgia. Their purpose was simple. First, break one of the brothers, Craig Olson, out of jail. All of us, with Dale's guidance, devised a plan to force that maneuver out of town. When they approach the car they thought Craig was in, they were asked to drop their weapons. Instead, they opened fire. In our own defense, we returned it. As you all know, it was a very foolish mistake on their part to start shooting when they weren't sure what they were firing at. All of our people wore body armor, which is why none of them died. Several of them have serious bruises where they were hit during the gun battle. None of the members of the criminal gang wore armor. They don't have bruises. And most of them are now dead."

The media people started to get restless, so Mack held up his hand to tell them to settle down. "The second part of their plan for us was to attack my home and kill me and my entire family. They particularly hated us because we were involved in shutting down most of their organization. As in the other raid, at the appropriate time they were told to put their weapons down and lay down on the ground. Again, they just opened fire. We returned it, and because of the plan Dale led us in devising, it was't much of a contest. Their survival rate was extremely low."

At this point, the very obnoxious reporter couldn't resist a comment. "I suppose," he said, his voice loaded with sarcasm, "your family was wearing body armor at the time?"

"Absolutely. To not wear it would be infinitely stupid."

"That hardly seems fair," mister obnoxious said. "They weren't members of law enforcement. Why should they be wearing that kind of protection? No one on the other side was."

Mack clenched the dais hard, gritted his teeth, and took several deep breaths to control his anger. He finally glared at the reporter. "I think that you're inferring that I should have put my family in additional danger. I should have put them in a position where they could have as easily as not been wounded of killed, in order to be fair, is so profoundly wrong, and downright sadistic, that it makes me sick. I've seen you media people sink pretty low sometimes, but this is the lowest. It's one thing to come here to report on a story so you can use the violence in it to kick up your ratings, but to twist it this way is going way too far."

Another reporter came up with a question every bit as bad. "I think you were asked a valid question," he said. "Weren't you putting your family's lives above all others?"

"No. No higher than the deputies who were with us. But higher than them scum of the earth who attacked us, absolutely. There are very few, if any, life forms existing on planet earth I don't, or wouldn't, rate higher than those monsters who attacked us. Do I feel bad that most of them are dead? Absolutely not. Was it wrong to provide my family with the best defense I possibly could. No! It was the most right thing I could do."

Another question. "You said you don't feel bad about the men who were killed. Don't you realize all human life is sacred."

"No. I am fully aware that there is way too much human life out there that is poison to the the rest of us. A lot of people have no redeeming qualities. They consistently do nothing but cause harm to everything around them. The men who came here from Georgia were such people."

This time the question came from a female. "You said you value most life forms higher than the men who died last night. Can you tell us which ones they are, and give us an example why?"

"I can't name them all, because there are so many it would take me most of the rest of the day to name them. If I could possibly remember them all, which I can't."

"Well then, tell us about one that is important right now."

"I'll tell you about three, then that will have to do it for now. I have a meeting that I need to go to this afternoon."

"I certainly hope your stories are about animals that matter. You could easily get boring."

"I thought I already was." Mack went on to tell them about the murder of Lisa's horses, Lancer, and the problems with the animal control man.

"You mean to say you protected a horse that actually killed a person?"

"I protected a good horse who only tried to defend his best friend and himself. The creature he was defending against had, among dozens of other crimes, recently raped and murdered a young girl. The idea that an innocent of any crime horse should be executed for trying to defend himself against that monster, was a definite miscarriage of justice. So I stopped it."

"It still seems to me, that a person's life is more important than the life of any animal, no matter what happened."

"That's because your value system is screwed up, and because you obviously know little to nothing about animals. And since you, and most everyone else in your group seem to feel the same, we might as well conclude this discussion now."

The female reporter spoke up again. "I can't speak for anyone else," she said, "but I would definitely like to hear your other story."

"Even if it isn't about last night?"

"Even then."

Most of the media people were still there, so he went ahead with the story about the bear. He began with the surprise encounter in the meadow behind their house, continued with what happened at the refuge.

With that part of the story done, he got into the serious part. "So even after the cubs play got us between them and their mama, she never made even the slightest aggressive move toward us. She just walked around us."

"What's the big deal about that?" A male reporter asked.

"Simple. Mother bears tend to be extremely aggressive when anyone or anything gets between them and their cubs. She wasn't, and that's the point for the rest of this story."

Mercifully, they let Mack continue. "The part of this story that illustrates the value of a given life form is this. Shortly after our encounter with the bear, two eighteen year old juvenile delinquent boys went into the refuge armed with twenty-two rifles. That's the first thing they did wrong. Weapons of any kind are not allowed on the refuge, without a special permit. They broke another rule when they killed a young doe. Only for the fun of it. They left the dead animal where it fell.

"Then, sadly, they met the bear. From their own admission, she and her cubs tried to leave the boys. The boys, thinking now that they were going to be real men, started shooting. They hit one of the cubs. That's when she turned on them. A bear can move a lot faster than most people realize. Those two morons were among the people who essential know nothing about wild animals. Other than they are something to shoot at and kill."

Mack paused to take a deep breath and to look out at his audience to see if any of them were actually listening. Most were, so he continued. "The bear, being bigger, stronger, faster, and most of all smarter than the boys, quickly caught them." There were a few chuckles when Mack mentioned the part about the Bear being smarter. "As anyone should expect, she did a pretty good number on the boys. What was surprising, was the fact she could have easily killed them. She didn't maul them near to the extent she could have either. It was almost as if she was saying that she wanted no more than to be left alone, and for her babies to be safe."

Mack just shook his head when he was interrupted again. "I still don't see any point to this. Is there one?"

"There is," a now very tired Mack answered. "And if you'll just shut the hell up for a while, I'll get to it." He glared at the reporter, and as he did, all heads turned in the same direction as Mack's. Mack continued with his story. "The point to the story is then, that the bear is innocent on any wrong doing of any kind. But according to some people in this community, the bear is guilty of being dangerously aggressive, and must be executed as soon as possible. Given how the event occurred, the boys should be punished, not the bear. And that brings me back to this idea that all human life is sacred. In this case, it's the bears life which is sacred, not the boys. And tired as I am, I'm going to the meeting this afternoon to argue for the bear's life. A life I consider to be worth every bit as valuable as the lives of those kids, if not a lot more."

Mack stopped talking then, and stood there waiting for a response. It came from one of the obnoxious reporters.

"So, you're actually claiming the bears life to be as valuable as the boy's?"

"At minimum. Truth is, it's worth more. All the bear wants is to live its life in peace, to exist while roaming from place to place, and only hunting when it's required. Those boys want to run around from place to place killing anything and everything that crosses their path. They want to do it without the slightest regard for the pain, for the damage, for the infinite cruelty involved in what they do."

"You make them sound like some kind of horrible creatures. They were just a couple of boys doing what boys do."

"The truth is, your comment about them being just a couple of boys doing what boys do is one to the single most stupid ideas humans everywhere have. I don't care how long *boys* have been doing what they do, that kind of behavior is wrong. And yes, it does lead to the kind of men who think it's their right to commit rape anytime they're in the mood. So I suggest you save that particular piece of bullshit for someone who might buy into it. 'Cause it sure as hell ain't me."

When Mack stopped talking, it stayed quiet for a moment. He decided then, that it was a good time to end the conference. Rather than say anything, he just turned his back and walked away. The stunned reporters let him go without screaming questions at his back.

CHAPTER 32

The meeting had already started when Mack got there. Several reporters were there, and more followed him when he went inside. Everything stopped as he moved to the front, picked a spot at one of the tables there, and sat down. He set the briefcase he carried on the top of the table, opened it, and took out the stack of papers inside.

He knew he was being closely watched, so he purposely moved slow. "You can resume the meeting," he said then.

The animal control person who wanted to kill Mack's horse, Dare, spoke up first. "You weren't invited to this meeting, Thomas," he said, "and we'd all appreciate it if you'd just leave. None of this concerns you."

"The truth is," Mack said, speaking softly and calmly, "it all concerns me. Number one among those concerns is people who think it is perfectly okay to invade the refuge while armed. It is not, and according to the special charter the refuge was granted when it became a private rather than public refuge, it not only is against the rules to do that. It is most emphatically against the law. I mention it now, so that everyone here is aware of the fact that if you decide you are going to hunt the bear down and kill it, whoever is designated to do it will be required to obtain a permit from the refuge board of directors. You should also know that I am currently head of that same board of directors." He smiled at mister animal control.

Animal control stood in front of the meeting, his face a brilliant red. He was angry. But it was one of the two boys who shot the bear cub who spoke up. "You have to let them kill the bear," he whined through the bandages on his face, placed there mainly for show. "It tried to kill us."

"If it had tried to kill you," Mack answered, "You'd be dead now. You and your buddy were the only ones trying to do any killing while you were in that refuge. You were lucky that bear was so gentle with you. Personally, I think you deserve more than you got."

One of the fathers stood, shook his fist at Mack, and yelled, "You sure are a lowlife bastard, saying a bear's life is worth more than my son's. I sure am glad our lawyer put your name in our lawsuit against the refuge."

"The same way I am glad to have your name on the refuge's lawsuit against you, your wife, and your son, and anyone in anyway involved in trying to do any kind of hunting on the refuge without a special permit."

"You don't stand a chance of beating us in court. We have a damn good lawyer."

"We have a damn good team of great lawyers. But even if, on the slim chance you win the domestic lawsuit, that's not going to change the fact that those bays who went into the refuge with the intent to kill as much as possible just for the pure hell of it, are going to jail. The refuge board has already decided to press charges against them. We will also be charging all the parents for aiding and abetting the crime. You might even get prison time for it."

"You sure are a vicious bastard, Thomas. You'd do all that to us only because our boys shot at a bear?"

"No, what you're doing goes way beyond two incredibly cruel, awesomely stupid, boys shooting a totally innocent bear cub. All the mother did was try her best to defend her babies. Now you want to kill her, even though the boys and you for giving them the guns, are the only ones guilty."

"But the bear is a danger to the entire community. It isn't safe with the animal running around loose." He pointed at the animal control officer. "He explained how bears, and all creatures like them, are dangerous."

"For the most part, they're only dangerous when we make them dangerous. The truth is, your son, as ignorant as he is, is a million times more dangerous with a gun in his hands than that mama bear could ever be. And as far as that particular animal control officer is concerned, he lives for the killing. He, in no other way, gives a good damn about your welfare."

"No matter what, I still don't understand why you're being so hard on my son?"

"It's simple, in the last day I have lived through hell. Somewhere around fifteen men died, ultimately because they were raised the way you're raising your son. Since I've been a sheriff's deputy, I've seen cruelty that goes beyond your imagination. I've seen people I loved murdered by people who started out the way your son has. And as bad as we treat each other, I still will never understand why we also have to hate the wild critters. Animals who mean us no harm. Yet constantly, human vermin like your son never stop the killing. I'm hard on him because I have absolutely no respect for him. I think he's a vicious little monster, and if he doesn't change, will grow up to be someone who beats his wife, then hates her for what he does."

As soon as Mack stopped talking, the three men in the front of the meeting came to life. The one in the middle, who happened to be a judge, used his gavel to get everyone's attention.

"I think," he said, "that this concludes this meeting." He banged his gavel again, dropped it, and with the other two, stood and left the room.

Mack still had no idea if he would win the war over the bear's life, but he knew he did win the first round. Dale, who should have at least be in his office taking it easy, met him on his way out.

"That was quite a performance, Mack. For a man who hates being in the public eye, you sure did get your point across."

Before Mack answered, he watched the people streaming passed him. He was surprised at how many of the reporters who went by, looked at him with a sympathetic eye.

He gave Dale a light smile when he answered him. "I hope you're right. It'll take a lot to save the bear. You know how much the public loves the drama of a good killing. Especially when it's a big, bad bear, or some such animal."

"That's true, but I've noticed, just standing here, that some of the reporters look like they might be on your side."

"I think some are, but I guess we'll just have to wait and see what they report."

They were surprised when the news stories started to come out. It was a close to equal mix of those in favor of the bear and those against it. There were even some that came across as being pretty much indifferent on the subject.

Because of the mixed reporting about the bear, there was no way they could be sure of its outcome. But Mack had to turn to other things. There were arrest warrants put out for Barry Olson, and Mack was the one chosen to deliver them to Georgia.

CHAPTER 33

Barry Olson was on the phone most of the day, searching for people to go to work for him. He was having a hard time finding any. The word had quickly gone out, over the little known online network that reported criminal activity, about the disaster the Georgia traffickers experienced when they went to Minnesota to teach the local law enforcement people a lesson. Since this disaster wasn't the first, but one of many, it was apparent to the criminal community that Barry Olson and the organization he controlled, would best be avoided.

By early afternoon, he'd given up for the day. It was now obvious to him that rebuilding his organization was going to be tougher than he initially anticipated. He'd always held himself aloof from his fellow criminals, because he considered himself to be far superior to them. So he was universally disliked by those same people he was now trying to recruit into what was without a doubt dangerous position.

He was also thoroughly disliked by his biggest customer, the Brazilian mining company who purchased most of the girls they acquired from the now defunct gang in Minnesota. He had no knowledge of their true attitude toward him though. From his own point of view, they liked him. Why would they not. For many years now, he had provided them with the highest quality women money could buy. And he was doing his best to put together a new supply for them.

So he was surprised when three of their representatives paid him a visit. He was somewhat concerned that they would do that, but still sure they could work out any problems that existed between them.

He wasn't quite so sure after the leader of the three asked the first question. "What's the status of the women we need to bring home with us?"

"There isn't any. I still need time to rebuild my organization. We were wiped out while we were up in Minnesota. It's just going to take some time."

"We don't have time," the man complained. "Those miners, they don't have much going for them, working out there in the jungle and other remote places. Women for them to fill their needs is one of the few things they have. They don't have women, they get restless. They don't work so hard then. They slow down and it costs us a lot of money. So if you ain't got no women for us, we ain't no longer got no use for you."

"All I need is time. I'll soon have all the women you can use."

"Not good enough. We need them now, so we'll be going to someone else for them."

"I'm sorry to hear that. But I'm sure we'll be doing business in the future. I'll be up and running before you know it."

"That might be possible," the one talking for the three said. "But you're a loose end now. Ours is a legitimate business and there's no way we can afford to take the chance you might develop a loose tongue."

"What the hell are you talking about?" Barry asked, not believing what he just heard. "In all these years, I've never given up anyone to the law. Not even the lowest of the lowest."

"That's what I've heard. But we can't take chances on there being a first time." He took his gun from its holster and leveled it at Barry's forehead. "Sorry about this," he said, actually sounding like he meant it. "But there ain't no choice this time."

Barry lifted his hand up in front of his face. "But I thought we always worked together real go..." He didn't finish.

The gun went off and he was instantly dead. It was suddenly too late for Mack, who was now on a plane headed for Georgia to arrest him.

When he got off the plane he rode a rail system for a long distance, then eventually climbed some stairs to an upper level. Standing there, near the top of the stairs, were two FBI agents. one held a small sign with his name on it.

They took him directly to their car. He sat alone in the back seat. "Do we have far to go?" He asked.

The agent sitting in the passenger side answered. "Not really. But the traffic's heavy tonight, so it'll take a while."

Mack didn't say anything more, so the agent who answered him turned back to face the front. Mack didn't mind the quiet at all, but he was surprised that neither agent had commented on his clothes. It was rare, when he was in new company, that he didn't get any questions about his dress.

He let himself relax on the ride, and had no idea where he was nor how he got there, when the passenger agent said, "We're on Price Road now, not that far from Gainesville. Not much farther, and we'll be at his mansion. When we get there, we're going to try to do this as peacefully as we can. But don't be surprised if we end up in a shooting."

"I won't," Mack said. "Up at my end of the world we've had way too many shootouts with people from his bunch."

"I would have thought it would be mostly peaceful up in that near empty part of the world where you live."

"There was a time," Mack told him, "when that's exactly what it was. But no more. Now we're doing what all the politicians and business people keep saying is most important. We're growing."

"What? You got something against that? Growth is what keeps the economy strong."

Mack knew from the man's tone that there was no room for a discussion, and even less point to an argument. Add to that, he was tired and only wanted to make the arrest, get on a plane with the man he came for, and fly home.

The entire grounds around the huge house Barry Olson lived in was now lit up, eliminating the evening shadows. They fully expected some kind of resistance when they knocked on the front door. It remained quiet, and no one answered the door.

After a second knock, they tried the door. It was unlocked, and they went in. They quickly found the body. Mack couldn't believe it. All the work they'd gone through to get this far, and the man was dead. A quick search of the mansion told them that the man was alone. Everyone one who had ever been with him was gone.

The first thing Mack did after the search was call Dale, to warn him that he'd be taking an earlier flight home. Then he did what he could to assist with the initial investigation, until the various crime scene people arrived.

He checked with the FBI guys to get their okay, then called a cab. While he waited he called the airport, got a seat on the next flight to Minnesota, and stood outside as he waited.

The flight home seemed long, and when the plane finally landed he was surprised but pleased to see that it was Lisa who was there to greet him.

She put her arms around him and kissed him before she said, "I can't tell you how happy I am to see you."

"I'm glad to see you too. But let's get the hell out of here and home," he told her. "I'm really tired."

"So am I," she agreed. "But we don't really have to be home tonight. So I booked us a room. A honeymoon suite actually. And that's where you and I are staying tonight."

Mack kissed her and said, "Show me where."

Tired as they were, they ate a decent room service meal in their room after showers. They then somehow managed to forget about sleep for a couple of hours.

They woke up once during the night, moved together, and it was another hour before they slept again.

For some reason, they were both tired when they met with Dale later the following day.

CHAPTER 34

After meeting with Dale and going over the events that brought an end to the Jackstone County/Gainesville, Georgia human trafficking syndicate, Mack and Lisa decided to take some vacation time. The first couple of days they stayed around home, helping Roy and Wanda with various tasks around their ranch.

They did anything from minor fence repair, to hauling and spreading manure on fields, to patching up a steer who managed to tangle himself in a barbed wire fence.

Evenings, they always took a walk through the meadow behind their house. They never tired of the scent of the native grasses as they walked through them. Watching all the life around them as they walked, brought further delight to their senses. And as always, the small herd of deer who now made the meadow their home, gave them a special joy every time they crossed paths with them.

It was a perfect Minnesota morning, with clear blue skies, a light breeze, and the temperature in the mid-seventies, that they decided to visit the refuge. Lisa was the first awake and out of bed that morning, and was enjoying a cup of coffee on their back deck when Mack joined her.

"Hi," she said, smiling broadly, "it's a perfect day."

"It is," he agreed, returning her smile. "A day for the refuge, I think."

"Me too. Right after breakfast."

They finished their coffee, got ready for the day, then walked the short distance to Mack's father, Ben's house. It was a solid tradition now, that Ben and his wife Theresa made breakfast for the family. Because of their jobs, Mack and Lisa were absent from far more of those breakfasts than they wanted to be. But they hadn't missed any with their time off, and found them a pure pleasure to be part of. Especially not having the pressure of rushing to the job.

Another thing that was so frequent that it was close to a tradition, was Mack and Lisa being the last to arrive at Ben's. That gave Roy the chance to make some kind of comment every day they were there for breakfast. This morning was no different. Lisa and Mack were still smiling when they arrived for breakfast.

"My, my," Roy said, "don't you two look chipper this morning. You must have something special planned for today."

Lisa loved to answer him with some kind of smart-assed comment, and this morning was no exception. "Actually, Roy, I had the whole day planned out. But Mack nixed it. He said he wasn't up to spending more than half the day in bed."

That filled the room with laughter. Roy laughed the hardest. He loved the way Lisa could frequently come back at him. Mack also loved her answer, and it brought him close to wanting to do exactly that. Half the day in bed with her would not be any kind of chore for him. Instead, he told them about their real plans for the day.

When he finished, Roy said, "Aren't you concerned about the bear? From what I hear every time I go somewhere, she's a dangerous killer. No place outside in Clayborne County is safe from her. And the refuge is sure death."

"I know. There's dozens of stories out there now about how she's attacked people. The thing is though, there's not even one shred of evidence to prove that any of the stories are true."

"You think then, Mack," Roy said, "that all those people telling the stories are liars?"

"I don't know what they are, other than stupid maybe."

"You're not worried about the bear then?"

"Not really. From what Lisa and I have seen from her, she's basically a gentle soul. All she wants is to live somewhere she's not constantly harassed by some two legged creature or another."

This time Ben spoke up. "Do you think, Mack," he asked, "that there's much chance you'll see her today?"

"A slight one maybe. She's sure to be a bit shy now, after losing one of her cubs the way she did."

"Well, if there's any chance of seeing her at all, I'd like to go along with you guys today. If you don't mind."

Mack loved the idea of bringing his dad along and said so. As soon as he did, Theresa said she wanted to go along too. Mack nodded his head yes, and quickly Roy and Wanda expressed the same interest. Sue Sartor joined them at the same time as Roy and Wanda. So after a very pleasant breakfast, the seven of them went to the refuge.

As people so often do in a group, they continued to talk as they went off down the trail they picked to hike. Mack was sure that their chatter, even though it was subdued, would be enough to keep the bear a good distance from them.

From his point of view, it didn't matter that much. The refuge's recovery from the fire, was alone reason enough to spend and enjoy a full day exploring.

Along with the recovery itself, the number of lifeforms now flourishing could satisfy most peoples wish for a fulfilling wildlife experience. And no one in this group was immune to the excitement when they watched a herd of twelve deer scatter when they approached them.

It proved to be the kind of day that satisfied their need to be out and among creatures whose only concern was living the life they were meant to have. It was nearly over, and they were on the last leg of the trail they were on, when she suddenly appeared in front of them.

The brush was growing prolifically there, and they didn't see her until she came around a bend in the trail. Mack happened to be in the front, and he raised his hand, telling everyone to stop. They did, and stood there silently watching a mama bear watch them.

She stood motionless, her cub safely tucked under her, between her front legs. She cocked her head to one side as she studied them, her knowing eyes telling them to not come any closer.

Mack, not at all sure what the best way to deal with her was, put out his hand, the same way he would for a strange dog. She shook her head at him, then made a sound that most would have taken as a growl. Mack knew there was no way he could be positive about it, but took the sound as a greeting. It was almost as if she was saying, "I know you. I've seen you before."

With that, she rose on her hind feet, gently waved both front paws in his direction, and dropped back down. Another slight shake of her head, and she turned her back to them. Ever so slowly, her body showing her total confidence as she moved, she walked back around the bend. It was time, she knew, to return to the place where she once lived. This bunch of those kind of animals were okay, but she knew she'd never be safe around most of them.

"What a vicious, dangerous animal," Mack said, his words filled with sarcasm.

"I guess," Ben said then, "we can all see now why you've always fought so hard for all the critters."

Lisa took his hand. "I wish," she said, "a lot more men could be like you."

"That's for sure," said Sue Sartor. "If you weren't already taken, I think I'd propose."

"What I'd like," Mack told them, "is that you'd forget about telling me how good I am, and do everything you can to protect all life we still have. We keep going the way we have been, it won't be long before it's gone."

If the bear was still there and could understand what he said, she would be in total agreement with him.

It was a satisfied group of seven people who left the refuge that day. Things were still a long way from perfect, but as long as there were places like this refuge, there was always hope for better times.

EPILOGUE

The Olson brothers reacted differently when they were told of their father's death. Craig had a fit of temper, and soundly cursed his father for letting him down. He considered his father's dying to be a direct stab in the back. He was sure the old man did it on purpose, only to make his life more difficult. He also suspected it was revenge for letting his brother get killed.

Jeff simply collapsed when he got the news. He knew, in that instant, that for all practical purposes his life was over. And to a large extent, it was.

Both brothers were found guilty of several counts of murder. They received a life sentence for each one. To be served consecutively. They ended up with even less hope when they were sent to different prisons.

*****

Mack and Lisa continued their search for a horse for her. They found the one she wanted at a medium size stable in western Minnesota. She was delighted to have finally found the horse that seemed to fit her wants and needs near perfectly. He was a pinto gilding, stood fifteen hands, and was both gentle and responsive. Even so, she didn't feel quite right as they drove the horse home in a trailer they owned.

"Somethings been bothering me, Mack," she said, "ever since we started looking for a horse for me."

"What? Are you worried about how he'll adjust to his new home?"

"No. I know that he and all the horses will have to make some adjustments. Maybe even fight some. But they'll work it out. And they'll do it better and faster than us humans ever do anything like that. They always deal with their social issues better than we do."

"What is it then? What's bothering you?"

"The horses we left behind. I know that most of them weren't being abused. Not directly anyway. But all too many were suffering from neglect. I just wish we could do something to make their life better."

"So do I. But we don't have the room for them. If we add more livestock, horses or cattle, to our ranch, we'll quickly be overcrowded."

"I know, Mack. And if we added more anyway, we'd become the neglectful ones."

"We would. But keep thinking about it, Lisa. You might come up with an answer yet."

*****

Two young men up in Jackstone County, who considered themselves to be as filled with as much machismo as two men could ever have, decided that the human trafficking business was just the thing for them, now that those previously in the business were now gone.

For several days they watched women come and go at a place called simply, 'The Women's Academy'. It was a place started during the worst of the human trafficking going on in the county. It was a place with with female members only, and few, if any males knew what it was. It kept the women off the street, and that's all most husbands and fathers cared about.

The two macho males thought it looked like a treasure house of victims they could use to start their new business. To start, they chose two very pretty sisters, only a year apart in age. They were the first women to join the academy, and were also the best students. They were good enough, in fact, to be planning to enter some future competition.

The macho men knew nothing about what the women were learning, and cared even less. Their plan for kidnapping the girls was simple. Walk up to them and grab them. Then drag them to their nearby car. It was a lousy plan. The sisters had been learning several different forms of self defense, and were already proficient at some of them. With little effort and several well timed moves, the macho two were quickly on the ground. The sisters, however, were knowledgable of ways of the world to not trust them or give them a break.

After the machos suffered several broken bones, the sisters called the police, who were told what the sisters expected the men to be charged with. Several weeks later, when they got out of the hospital, they were convicted of the crimes they were charge with. They are both trying to learn a trade as they do their time in prison.

*****

Mack was patrolling one of the county roads around the refuge on one of his restless early mornings, when he noticed a pickup parked on the side of the road. It was no ordinary truck. This was a special truck, designed for use by animal control.

Mack suspected it was the same animal control person who was so anxious to kill his horse, Dare, and was equally determined to kill the bear. It was early enough in the day for the grass and other vegetation to be covered with dew, so tracking the man was easy.

Mack found him sitting with his rifle resting on a downed oak, once blackened by the fire but now washed clean. Off in the distance a coyote stood, looking for a meal in the grass.

It was more that Mack was about to allow. Without warning, he reached over the man, grabbed his riffle, and yanked it out of his hands. He turned the gun on the man and asked, "You anxious to die today?"

"What the hell you talking about. You got no right to take my gun away from me."

"Truth is," Mack said, "I have every right to do a hell of a lot more than take your gun. Now get off your ass before I fix it so you can't. This is my territory, and you damn well will do what you're told."

"I will not. You don't have any authority over me."

"You have broken several of the rules concerning this refuge. Bringing a gun into it without a permit is just one of them. It's the worst, but only one. You are now officially under arrest. You are going to jail."

Animal Control objected all the way to the sheriff's office, but Mack ignored him. As soon as he had the man locked up, he called the company that provided a towing service and had Animal Control's truck hauled to the impound lot.

Mack then did all of the required paperwork, and before the day was over a court date was set. And if Mack had his way, there would be some jail time for the man who so loved to kill defenseless animals.

*****

It was a rare Minnesota morning. The weather was perfect. It was Saturday, and Mack and Lisa were relaxing on their back deck, enjoying a cup of coffee as they watched life unfold in the small meadow that started in their back yard.

"We are two incredibly lucky people," Lisa said, "to have all this. I know how great the refuge is, but look what we have right here. Out there in that meadow, we have our own refuge life and home. How could anyone ask for more than what we have."

"No one could. but we have even more than just that."

"What could that be, Mack?"

"Each other."

www.ingramcontent.com/pod-product-compliance
Lightning Source LLC
Chambersburg PA
CBHW070539100726
47907CB00004B/1184